Binding of the Almatraek

Book Two:

Noble Pursuit

Written By

Heather Reilly

Published by Reillybooks

ISBN-13: 978-0991936724

ISBN-10: 0991936728

Acknowledgments

I would like to thank, my husband for always treating my writing seriously. Though I am actually a teacher by trade, he always made me feel as though the books I write are just as important, and I couldn't ask for more support than that.

I would also like to thank the Levine family for their care, and as my second family, their love as well. If it weren't for their kindness and interest in this project, I would never have had the guts to keep trying to get the series published. Thanks also to David, who took hours to sit with me and use his keen eye to make the whole series better. He made me think, and forced me to become a better writer.

Lastly, I would like to thank my father, who to this day still makes me feel like "Daddy's little girl". You have always made me feel like any endeavor I undertake is of worth, no matter how large or small.

Other books by the author:

Binding of the Almatraek
Book I: Knight's Surrender

The Tree and the Sun

Upcoming books:

Binding of the Almatraek
Book III: Enchanting Page

Tock Tick Tock,
The Mouse and the Clock

All titles are available at
www.reillybooks.com

This book is dedicated, as always, to my husband.

This book is also dedicated to my Newfoundland fan base. I hope you love this book as much as the first that swept you away.

As a side note to my younger readers, Newfoundland is a breathtakingly beautiful island on the eastern tip of Canada. If you haven't been there, go! The people are the best and kindest you will meet in the whole world, and the island is rich with experiences you might not find at home.

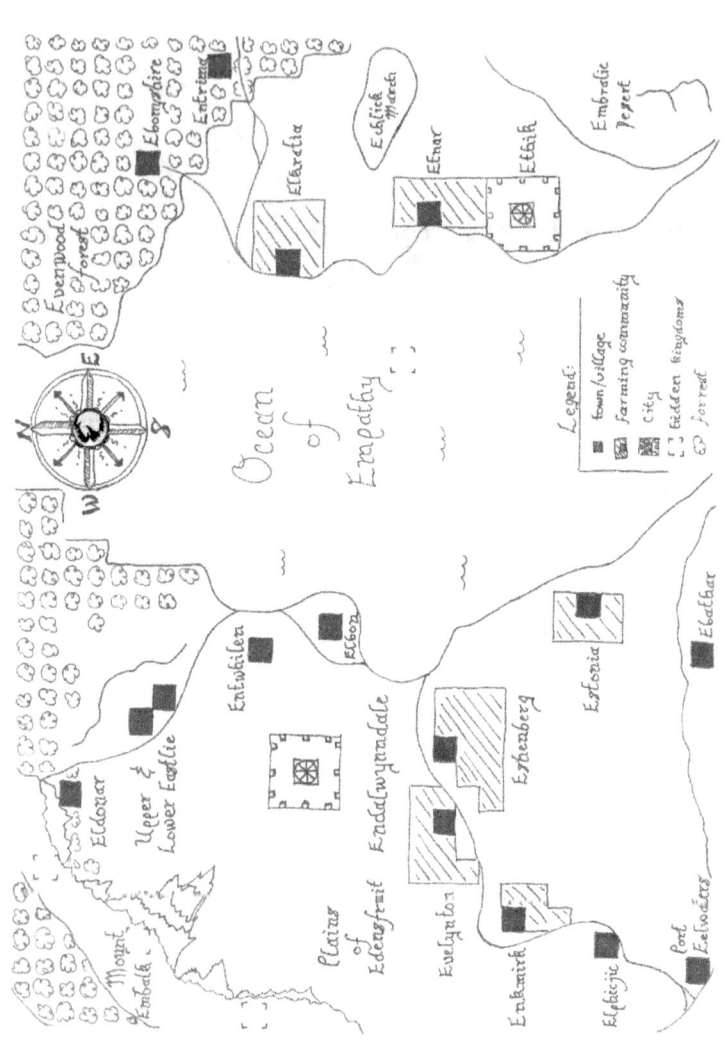

Chapter 1
~ Knight's Rescue ~

deafening roar of approval washed over the palace, filling the air with energy until it seemed to vibrate with the sound. The past few moments had been silent and tense, but the announcement of Aylan coming to light as Oslan's mage had evidently been received well by the crowd. It never failed to impress Oslan when royalty assembled the population to speak. Although there were hundreds of bodies present, as they waited eagerly to hear the news, he believed he would be able to hear a pin hit the smooth stones beneath their feet should one happen to fall.

The peasants and nobles alike happily looked on and cheered, squinting up at the balcony in the bright warm sunlight as a couple of servants set to the task of releasing seven white doves into the air. As they flew, Aylan found the pool of energy at her centre and cast a spell: "Tur aweya," *Change colour.* This was one of her newer spells that made the doves' white downy feathers morph into a myriad of hues. The rainbow of birds circled low over the square as children sitting upon their parents' shoulders eagerly stretched up their hands in an attempt to snatch one of the magnificent fowl out of the air. The doves spiraled higher and higher, causing their shadows to race over the faces of the onlookers currently lost in wonderment. Finally, the doves changed back to pure white in a flash and soared off into the late afternoon sky.

Oslan, the young man slated to become the next king of Endalwynndale, stood beside his new mage and marvelled at the dramatic change she had undergone in the past year. His affection for her had grown ever since the day she had first been brought before him when he had been only twelve years of age. She had come to the castle from a farm, used to chores and dressing in boy's clothing, a habit that she still hadn't left behind since coming to live in the castle to be trained by the former king's mage. Almost his height when they met, she had continued to sprout up, and her hair left forgotten had grown out. Her hair was now arranged into intricate blonde braids and curls, and she sported for the first time an elegant gown made of gossamer turquoise. She turned to him and smiled, catching his eye in a way that made him remember the intimate kiss they had shared not ten minutes before stepping out onto the balcony where they now stood. The past years of working closely together had not only transformed her into his mage, but also the object of his heart, making his parents attempt to quash the relationship with the common girl several times. He was to be king after all, and must therefore by law marry a noble. His parents would never hear of him marrying one of his lesser subjects, and a farm-girl at that. Suddenly feeling shy, he shifted his gaze back to the peasants below.

The breeze that carried his subjects' cheers up to them also brought the smell of the noble ladies' colliding perfumes, and ruffled Oslan's hair. His only regret right now was that his father was not here to see this moment. *He would have been so proud,* thought the prince in sorrow, remembering the king's recent death. Ideally, Oslan would have taken the throne after the king had died, however, right now the queen was ruling in his stead until his coronation. The law of the land stated that any ruler of Endalwynndale must first be wed. This was partly to ensure that there would always be an heir to the throne. If the kingdom were to have a king that was not married, he may choose to live out his life without a wife, precluding him from having children in the public eye, and therefore, no legitimate heir.

After finally falling in love, Oslan's father had at first forbade him from marrying his mage. She was deemed unsuitable due to her common upbringing and the scandalous way that she insisted on continuing to wear boy's tunics, even after years of living in the castle for her training. At a recent ball, Aylan's powers had allowed her to create an illusion of a beautiful woman, which was introduced to the king as a noble with Aylan's name. The king had been smitten with the image. He had willingly given his permission for them to wed, thinking that she was a much better choice for the prince than the peasant that had been standing nearby that dressed like a boy. Less than an hour later, the king had been killed by poison added to his wine during the toast to their engagement. Oslan had put off the wedding long enough to pursue the villainous mage that had created the plot to overthrow their kingdom. He now sat locked in a tower high above the keep, in a solitary room with pouches packed into the brickwork of the walls that ensured that he was devoid of magic. *It is so unfair,* Oslan thought with a quiet rage, *that I should have to pay for the man's upkeep that killed my father.*

Oslan decided to turn his thoughts back to the moment at hand before his ponderings could sour the occasion with grief. Aylan turned to him while waving at the crowd and noticing something was amiss, placed a warm hand on one of his broad shoulders. Her smile was infectious, and he found himself smiling warmly back at her despite his gloomy thoughts.

"Shall we retreat before they start making

requests?" She asked in good nature. Oslan nodded, and with a final wave and the kingdom's salute of placing an opened hand over his heart, he took her arm to lead her back inside the palace.

Upon re-entering the hallway, they were met by a flustered stocky servant wearing the castle's familiar grey-brown livery. "Your mother, the queen, wishes to see you, Your Highness," he delivered. Once the message was conveyed, the servant bowed low and removed himself from the hall.

One of the knights standing guard inside the balcony stepped forward. Oslan recognized him as Carn, one of his most trusted knights. Though he was older than Oslan by almost two decades, Oslan had trained and voyaged with Carn for years, and he considered him to be one of his closest friends. "If it pleases, I shall accompany you, Sire," said Carn, "I also have business to discuss with the queen." Oslan nodded in consent and he, Aylan and Carn set off in the direction of the throne room where the meeting would take place.

Carn strode surely beside the prince, wearing his gleaming armour as always. He held the familiar helmet with its comb of blue fur under his arm. His blue velvety cape rustled lazily as he walked, his boot heels kicking it out at the back as they proceeded down the hall. His thick combed-back blond wavy hair sat just above his shoulders, in contrast to the dark hair of the prince that was just starting to curl above the prince's ears. Walking side by side, they looked to be very similarly built, though for the occasion, the prince wore no armour. A year ago, Carn had been almost a head taller than the prince, but now Oslan had grown until they were almost equals in both height and stature.

They walked along the opened upper hallway that ran all the way around the keep, and where they could look down over the marble railing onto the floor below. Side by side, they passed pillars and lavish tapestries until they rounded the corner to the far corridor that would take Aylan to the wing of the castle that housed her chamber. Soon enough, she would be permitted to attend these royal family discussions as well, but until the prince and she were married, she was technically still just his mage. *My mage and my fiancée,* the prince thought proudly, *soon to be my wife and queen.* Aylan left him then to go attend to her handmaid and confidante, Millie. Now that the announcement had been made that put her in the public light, she would be expected to wear a gown whenever she appeared in court. Oslan had urged her to go shopping in the marketplace for new material that the royal tailor could then make into gowns fit for the queen she would be. Never the fancy sort, she had agreed to go, but grudgingly so.

Oslan and Carn carried on to the throne room that sat at the back of the palace. As they approached, Oslan held back a step, allowing his older friend to pull the heavy oak doors outward so they could enter. Once through, they walked along the red carpet runner that led to the thrones. Oslan walked a step ahead, taking the position of power, but Carn kept close behind so that they could still speak as they walked past the courtiers and guards that adorned the throne room. "Have you heard rumours of what this might be about?" Oslan asked over his shoulder in a hushed tone.

"I haven't a clue, Your Highness," was Carn's murmured response.

"I told you to call me Oslan, Carn. Even though you watched me grow up, you are still my closest friend and brother in arms" Oslan insisted impatiently not for the first time.

"And after the small matter of a little marriage ceremony of Endalwynndale's only prince, you will be my king as well." Carn pressed, "You had better get used to formality, my Liege." Oslan only sighed heavily as a response, resigning himself to the decorum that would mark the rest of his life.

They stopped in front of the dais, Oslan tilting his head in recognition, and Carn bowing low before the queen. Oslan waited expectantly in front of his mother, remaining on the crimson runner before the stairs since she had requested the audience. Once their business was concluded, he would ascend the five stairs that would bring him to his throne at her side.

"Welcome, my son, and you too, Sir Carn," Queen Elsa greeted them. She wore a deep purple gown today that was secretly Oslan's favourite. She had worn a gown of the same colour when he was a young child, and his fond memories of the hours he spent with her were triggered by the colour now. Her dark hair shimmered in the light at the slightest movement of her curls, and the crown she had chosen for this occasion was tall and pointed in its dainty twists of jewel encrusted metal. She chose this crown whenever she wanted to accent her ruling power. Since she had worn it for him today, it told him that this was to be a discussion where she would likely exert her role as queen over any argument he made. He itched to have this over with, it was bound to be unpleasant.

"Quite a miraculous transformation," the queen allowed, "She really has become a beauty, when she is not dressed as a boy."

Oslan's glance hit the floor as he realized that the queen had made the connection that the lady who had been announced as his fiancée was the same girl that had been denied him by the recently passed king. He quickly tried to recover, hoping that his mother had not caught the flash of guilt that had momentarily shone on his face.

"Yes, she is beautiful, Mother," he agreed in defiance, "and my father thought as much as well. He felt she was worthy, and gave his permission for us to be wed at the ball. There is nothing to discuss."

In reaction, the queen stood and addressed the room: "I am afraid that I must invite all of you to return after the noon repast. My son and I have much to discuss in private." Among mumbles of acquiescence and quieter grumbles of complaint, the nobles present slowly filed out of the throne room. Once the last courtier had quitted the room, and the guards present had barred the door behind them, Queen Elsa regarded her son for a long while and continued.

"Despite how you appeared to have produced a new girl altogether, she is still just a farm girl, and the law of the land still exists. No matter how she looks Oslan, you may not marry that far below your station. You should be marrying a princess to join our kingdoms and extend your lands."

"But Mother, I love her," he said placidly, already feeling the sting of defeat over this matter once again.

"This I know Oslan. I have known since I first saw you in the same room together. Nothing about my children escapes my notice." She thought about his clever trick at the ball, and added, "for too long."

"Your Highness?" Carn addressed her from behind Oslan. Both the queen and prince turned to see which of them he was referring to. With his face turned toward Queen Elsa, Carn continued, "I know it is not my place to interfere, that as a knight I am to be the eyes, yet not the ears of the discussions that take place in this room. However, may I have permission to speak? I feel that I may be able to aid in this particular situation." With that he bowed low in front of the Queen to show the utmost respect though he spoke out of turn.

"Speak," she granted him, "but take care of your words Carn, for the other eyes in the room may yet have ears too."

Carn nodded and raised himself from his bow. He took a few moments to collect his thoughts, choosing his words carefully. "If I understand Majesties, Oslan must marry a lady, someone of noble blood, yet his betrothed's bloodline is untested?"

"She is a farm girl, a peasant of no consequence. On the royal tapestry her farm has no coat of arms." The Queen confirmed.

Carn directed his next question at Oslan: "At the ball, your father introduced her as Aylan Suresword, is that her true name?"

"Yes, she told me that her father was a knight of this kingdom. But unfortunately, being the daughter of a knight doesn't grant you nobility. When the knight falls, as her father did, the title dies with him."

"This is true Sire, I fought alongside him in my youth, he was a great swordsman." Carn confirmed.

"What is the point of all this Carn? I grow weary of talk of swordplay, we are discussing the fitness of my son's choice of bride." The Queen interjected.

"Forgive me, Your Highness," Carn apologized, "It is just that there was more to Elgan Suresword than his position as a knight. He was in fact the son of the former Duke and Duchess of Eldonar. When he started as a knight, he was actually the Lord of Eldonar. His family held dual lands, as the duchess had previously been the Lady of Eshenberg. Being the elder child in the family, the higher title passed to him and upon the deaths of his parents, he became the Duke of Eldonar, brother of the Countess of Eshenberg."

"That means-" Oslan began, but was interrupted by the queen that confirmed for him the words that were on the tip of his tongue.

"She *would* be nobility. The Lady of Eldonar, in fact." She said pensively, "It is curious that she and her mother, the Duchess of Eldonar, did not insist on such introductions at the feast before the tournament. Also, I find it interesting that she did not attend the ball given your bold announcement about her daughter. Go to the Duchess, Carn. Find out exactly why she has been hiding her title. Oslan, I would ask you to seek Aylan out and demand the reason that your mage has been deceiving you."

<

Chapter 2
~ Fame from Flames ~

Oslan appeared at Aylan's door within minutes of his interview with the queen, hoping that his intended had put off her trip to the market. He knocked softly and waited impatiently for her response. After a few moments, with gradually more persistent knocking, he gave up and went to see if she had instead gone to do some work in Lazelan's laboratory. *Hers,* he mentally corrected himself, *it's her laboratory now.* He reached the hall that held the armoury and war room beyond, and laid his hand over his heart to give the door guards the royal salute. They motioned back to him and stood aside, allowing him to pass through the heavy oak double doors. He stopped to appreciate the majestic sword that gleamed as a centre piece on the wall.

With a jet black and braided gold hilt, the sword Skirdkhen, sat upon an ornate wooden wall mount. The dragon's fire insignia that adorned all of the knight's armour in Endalwynndale was also inlaid into the hilt where the cross-guard met the grip. The blade, with one wavy edge and the other serrated, was always sharp despite the generations that it had remained in Oslan's family. Finally, a fire breathing dragon was etched into the length of the blade, its fire brushing the tip of the sword. This was no ordinary weapon: it was the symbol of peace in Endalwynndale, and whenever it struck, it left behind the hot scorch marks of fire.

Oslan gingerly let his fingers pass over the dragon, feeling the bumps and ridges of the pattern along the blade before stepping back to continue on his way. He thought about the power of the sword, now his birthright, as he left the armoury through a side door. His next steps took him into the war room, where a massive oak table and heavy chairs spread across most of the available space. A huge tapestry hung on the side wall in this room. It served as decoration, a map of the kingdom, and as cover for a secret passageway built into the wall behind it. Every piece of land in the kingdom was depicted by the thick woven threads, and each bore the coat of arms of the lord or lady that was in charge of the property. Aylan's farm stood just to the right of the middle of the tapestry, with no coat of arms. Oslan looked north to Eldonar and saw the coat of arms of the Duke. On it, a majestic griffin stood reared, talons clawing at the air, and a sword and shield held the opposite quarter. Seizing the edge of the tapestry, the prince circled around it and disappeared into the passageway that only he and three others knew about.

He hastened through the dark stone corridor, making a mental note to get Aylan to cast a spell to get rid of some of the cobwebs that hung lazily here and there where the ceiling touched the walls. *Honestly,* he thought to himself with annoyance, *how do spiders survive in here anyway, there can't be anything to eat. It's a secret passage, not a pig pen ripe with flies!* He ducked under a particularly low hanging web and shuttered. He wasn't afraid of spiders, but he also could not brag about liking them overly. They just sort of gave him the heebie-jeebies. *It's a good thing they don't bother Aylan. Although I suppose if they did they would have been cleared out of here long ago.*

He followed the guiding edges of the door, which was framed in flickering candle light from within the workroom ahead. Soft female voices reached his ears. *She hasn't gone to the marketplace then after all,* the prince reflected with a sigh, *I'm afraid I may have to take her there myself if I am to get her to go.*

A musical laugh coming from beyond the door told him that Sasha was Aylan's other visitor. Sasha's gift was as secret as this laboratory. Many people had noticed her and asked for introductions on account of her beauty, however, her talents were hidden from almost everyone in the kingdom. She was his seer, and a good one at that. Since a young age, she had had the ability to read people and see the future in dreams, and had in fact, saved her whole village from burning before she had reached the tender age of three.

The prince reached the door and entered without knocking. Disturbing a lady in her private chambers required a certain amount of respect and decorum, but throughout the rest of the castle, Oslan had free rein. As the girls heard the latch, Sasha beamed, "Ah, there he is now." Aylan brightened as he entered, and the prince felt warmth spread through his chest for her. *Brightness she's beautiful, and to think that I can make her face light up like that.* He remarked. The two girls were seated at the high square wooden table in the middle of the tiny room. The walls were covered by shelves stocked with vials, jars and pouches of various herbs and ingredients for Aylan's herbology.

When Oslan had found her, she had been quite adept at the art already. Herbology was the skilled labour of mixing herbs and other matter found in nature to create chemical reactions that would produce different effects. For example, she almost always carried a small pouch of a flameroot powder at her waist. He got to see the effects of that plant the day that he had first noticed Aylan far below his window in the marketplace. He had watched a thief steal some jewelry and watched as Aylan's fingers deftly flicked some of her pouch's contents onto the man's feet, which promptly set his shoes ablaze. The thief leapt into a nearby horse trough to douse the flames, and the merchant's things were returned. Oslan had laughed out loud in amusement and approval. He had immediately sent Carn to bring the girl for an audience with him. Thinking that she had been in trouble for causing the fire, she had run off, forcing Carn to pursue her across the land all the way to her home. Only once she had been cornered there had she stopped long enough to find out what he wanted.

Oslan looked at her now, filled with amusement at the memory, and a slight chuckle escaped his lips that gave his thoughts away. The two ladies could almost feel the change in his thoughts as his smile slowly faded, and he remembered why he had come to interrupt Aylan's work.

"What has happened?" Sasha began in her light clear voice, "All sunshine one moment, and sombre the next. This can't be good news."

←

Chapter 3
~ His Story, A Fascinating Subject ~

"I'm afraid I must speak with Aylan alone Sasha. I know you may search out the reason why on your own, but I would ask you not to until I give you leave to do so," Oslan requested.

"Of course, Oslan," Sasha assured him.

"Aylan, will you walk the gardens with me?" He asked while holding out his hand to her to help her off of her high stool. Aylan and Sasha exchanged a glance.

"Go on," Sasha encouraged, "I'll clean up here."

Looking back at Oslan, Aylan agreed to go by taking the prince's offered hand and allowing him to lead her out the door.

"So, I like what you've done with the place here," Oslan joked as they passed under the cobwebs. Being royalty, Oslan was expected to be obeyed by his subjects, but he tried to hint to Aylan about the condition of the corridor without directly ordering her to clean it up. Her eyes flicked up to meet his briefly before she muttered something under her breath in Almatrae, the language that the mages used to command their magic energy. At once, a gust of wind swept up the hall, taking with it all of the cobwebs and leaving the corridor bare.

"I hope I don't have any spiders roosting on my tunic now from back down the hall," he half joked.

"Ha ha," she laughed sarcastically in response, but it wasn't an answer. Oslan deftly leaned back to get a view of the back of her gown. He assumed that since they had both been brushed by the same gust, that his clothes would look the same as hers. It was clean. Inwardly, he sighed with relief.

A comfortable silence spun out between them, and his thoughts turned to Carn as he walked. Before his father had died, the prince had found his friendships with nobles, knights, and commoners alike easy. Part of the reason Oslan's subjects loved him so, was that he treated everyone, right down to the lowly peasant children, with respect. People came away from encounters with him with a sense of pride, joy, and a feeling of self-importance because he had taken the time to stop to talk to them as a real person, and not as property.

Now that he was to be king though, with his coronation only pending his marriage to Aylan first, he was finding it more difficult to keep these easy conversations going. Now people were bent on pomp and humility whenever they met their would-be ruler. He still wanted those close to him, those he considered to be true friends, to feel that they were being given requests as opposed to demands. He loathed the fact that Carn had become overly formal when addressing him, although Oslan recognized that this was Carn's way of hinting to him how important it was to have him on the throne.

The prince and his mage stopped behind the tapestry that hung across the secret entrance, listening for voices or movement. Satisfied that the room beyond was empty of prying eyes, the couple emerged from behind the heavy red and green coarse fabric. They walked together, a hand's breadth apart, through the castle and down to the gardens below. Going out into the cool evening air, the sweet scent of the roses, lilacs and other flowers on the bushes floated to them on the soft breeze. Crickets chirped loudly from the expanse of lawns between each portion of the garden, setting a peaceful mood as the sun finished setting behind the tall castle wall. "I love that sound," Aylan sighed as she closed her eyes to drink it in.

"I can think of one that's better," the prince responded.

"What's that?" she enquired, while once again regarding him.

"Call me crazy," he replied, "but I love the sound of your voice, especially when I listen to you cast.

"You like listening to me use magic?" She asked, surprised, "Why?"

"I think I just like the sound of your voice speaking a language that is foreign to me," he said, "I find it intriguing and beautiful." He told her honestly. But it was time to get to the matter at hand. "I'm afraid I have received some serious news that we must talk about." Aylan stopped walking and faced him, alarmed. He took both of her hands in his and led her to a stone bench nestled in an alcove of peach coloured rose bushes on a patch of grass. The stars and moon had begun to shine in the now darkened sky. He regarded her, and watched as a small gust of wind caused some of her stray blond hair to flutter around the edges of her face. Oslan said a silent prayer and closed his eyes to collect his thoughts. *How do I broach the subject? How do I start? Should I just tell her she's a lady and watch for her reaction, or should I ask her why she kept it from me? Help me to make this go well. I love her as my second half and don't want to lose her.*

Taking a deep breath, he delicately encouraged: "Tell me about your father."

"What does my father have to do with anything?" She asked, startled. "He's been gone since I was a young child."

"Please," he urged, "tell me everything that

you know about him."

"Well," she started, "he was a knight that served your father. He was on patrol at our kingdom's eastern boarder when he saved some travelling traders from a band of marauders. In thanks, they gave him a warning, and supplied him with the location of a noble that was rumoured to be able to cast, and had been collecting evil spells within the kingdom. He had kept his activities a secret, and when my father reported the news to the king, he was almost thrown in the dungeon for speaking out against a noble without having proof. For some reason, something my father said struck a chord with the king, and he managed to avoid any punishment. Perhaps if he had been locked away, he would still be alive today." She continued quietly.

Oslan could see her eyes begin to glisten with tears that refused to spill over. He still held her hands as they sat knee to knee, and he gave them a reassuring squeeze. "I am sorry, I can see how difficult this is for you, but please go on." He gently pushed.

Taking a deep stuttering breath in and out, she continued, her voice beginning to crack in her grief. "King Eurilas sent him with a small group of other knights to investigate my father's claims. They travelled south to Ebathar, where the noble, a man by the name of Lord Meltrabus resided. My father never made it back. Mother hasn't told me more than that." She continued, a sad smile touching her lips. "Whenever I pressed her, she always told me that it is a story unfit for a lady's ears. It's at that point that I tell her that no one has ever accused me of being a lady, so she should tell me anyway, but it never works."

It pained Oslan to see the sadness in her, but

he didn't yet have the information he needed to confirm or deny Carn's assertion. He pressed on: "What do you know of your father before he met your mother?"

"Not much," Aylan admitted while slowly shaking her head, "just that my parents met while my father was on his way to see his sister in Eshenberg. It was winter, and he and three others had been riding for days when he saw my mother's cottage in the snowy fields. He drove his horse toward the flickering candle light he saw by the window. She claims that he always said that it felt like coming home. He wasn't travelling alone and my mother's home is small, yet she fed them all and let them warm themselves by the fire.

He was impressed by her generosity, and willingness to help out a band of complete strangers. Mother swears up and down that it was really due to her cooking, that after they were hosted for the night and continued on their journey, my father returned to see her on his way back to his own home. They courted through letters for a time, and then they got married. He wanted her to come live with him, and she did, for a time, anyway. They were in love, and happy, and I was born a year later.

I was only six months old when my father left to go on the mission for the king. After his death, mother went back to her old house. She said that the other place just didn't seem like home without him there, though she still keeps in touch with people from her time there, and still goes to visit quite often. That's why I was so self-sufficient, I used to be sent away to my aunt's when she was away, however when I got older, she left me to tend the farm in her absence. It's thanks to the coin I've made here that I've been able to send her money for a servant in my stead."

Oslan pondered this. "Tell me, where was your father from?"

"I don't really remember," she shrugged, "Eldonar, or one of the Eastlies or something."

"Your mother never told you." It was a statement, not a question from the astonished prince.

"Well, she did, but I tend to forget the details. I remember that it was north of here, that's got to count for something." She said more jokingly. "If you want to know for sure, you should ask Carn. They went on the same mission together for King Eurilas and became fast friends. Mother said that my father even mentioned him in a few of the letters that he sent back while posted in Ebathar. It was Carn that eventually sent word of Father's death, and servants to return my father's shield and sword. That was the day we moved back to mother's cottage from where they used to live. I don't remember it at all, I was only an infant at the time."

The prince sat for a moment, digesting this. As long as his mage was being honest, and he thought she was, his curiosity was satisfied. He wondered if her mother would tell the same story. Now he just needed confirmation from Carn.

←——

Chapter 4
~ Conforming for Confirmation ~

Carn returned to the neat cottage where he had first sought out Aylan for the prince almost two years before. He remembered the jewelry the overjoyed merchant had bestowed upon him to bring to her. It had been bracelet of horsehair with two turquoise beads, which she still wore to this day.

That was before the girl knew magic existed and was only skilled in the arts of farming and herbology. Carn reflected that herbology in itself was an impressive skill to have. Many things akin to magic could be accomplished with it if one only knew the right plants to mix to make draughts, pills, powders and ointments that could seem to achieve miracles. He and his horse had been privy to a dose of flameroot powder that she had thrown on the path to slow their pursuit. Her mother must be sorely missing this talent while her daughter resided at the castle.

He had ridden up to the house that day much as he had today, though today's ride had been at a much slower pace. Now knowing whose house this was, the memory of his good friend made him approach the door with a certain sense of reverence. He dismounted, leaving his horse to graze while he stepped up to the doorway. He could hear a pretty voice singing from inside. The swishing sounds of a broom whisking across wood floors occasionally drowned out the lower notes emerging through the opened window. Taking a deep breath, he raised his gauntleted fist and knocked heavily three times, causing dust to rise up off the wooden door.

Inside, the whisking sound stopped, and a musical "Coming!" reached his ears. The door swung inward, and Carn came face to face with the cheery features of Aylan's mother, Lorelyn. She still looked much the same way she had the day he collected Aylan and whisked her away to meet Prince Oslan. Today, she donned a coarse grey skirt, which swayed around her body as she stepped back to make room for him to enter her comfy home. She had been plump two years ago, but now he noted that her skirt floated slightly around her hips, and that her bodice was laced as tight as it would go, yet was still a little too loose as if she had lost weight but had not bothered to buy or sew new clothes. Her curly blonde hair was tamed into a bun, just as it had been the last time they met. Her look was very different than it had been all those years ago when Elgan had been alive, but this *was* his old friend's wife. She used to wear her hair loose, and was only a scrap of a girl, which may have been why he hadn't recognized her in his haste to get Aylan to the castle two years prior. She had still retained her vivacious nature, to his relief.

"Hello, Sir Carn, I was wondering when you'd come again." She declared, offering him a seat with her hand while she spoke.

"Thank you, but you needn't be so formal," he replied. She waved his comment off as he looked about the late afternoon sunlight-filled cottage for a place to sit. As before, it was a tidy space, with pots and pans hanging from one wall beside a large cooking hearth, which was now dark except for a few glowing embers amongst white feathery ashes. His boots thumped dully on the floor made of earth and stone as he crossed to the only visible seats: benches along the table. He instinctively sat with his back to the wall, which gave him a view of the whole room and the doorway.

"You remember me." It was a statement, not

a question. In his younger years, his cheeks would have coloured with the chagrin he felt at this. He had at first overlooked her during his last visit to the cottage. He could see how her true identity could easily been hidden. These surroundings suited her, she was happy here, and she held herself not as a duchess, but as a commoner.

"By the shields of the army of Ormond, Carn, of course I remember you," She said with an air of impatience, "it's not every day that a knight comes to my home and takes my daughter away!" She started gathering a small pile of wood into her arms and continued, "Let me just relight the fire and I'll set about heating some water for tea." She began to pile the kindling in the hearth, and was startled to hear the jingle of Carn's chain mail, followed by the keen scent of him as he knelt beside her.

"Let me help you with that," he insisted, taking the timber out of her hands. As he moved to take the wood, his fingers brushed hers for a brief instant. He cleared his throat and she quickly straightened, flattening the white apron over her skirts with her hands before retreating to the wall of pots. He set about bringing the flames to life from the embers while she collected a pot of water and positioned it over the new fire. Then they moved to sit across from each other, the simple wooden table spanning the tiny distance between them.

"I will have to get Aylan to make me a new batch of tea when next she visits," Lorelyn observed, "I fear I will soon run short, and my strength in herbology goes no farther than cooking a good meal."

"If not taught by her mother, how else would a lady pick something like that up?" ventured Carn. Lorelyn's brown eyes flicked up to meet Carn's steady blue ones at the title he used.

"This young lady," she corrected, "learned about herbology while summering with her aunt. There was a gardener there that was very knowledgeable in the science, and he took her under his wing."

"While she was summering with her aunt..." Carn let his voice trail off.

"Yes," Lorelyn replied coolly.

"That would be the Countess of Eshenberg, would it not?" Carn questioned. "Aylan has mentioned her before."

"It would be," was Lorelyn's wary reply, "but that is in the past. Now, it is neither here, nor there."

"Elgan's younger sister." Carn pressed, "Or am I wrong?" Lorelyn removed herself from the situation by getting up to make the tea. She set the steaming brew before them and turned to retrieve some baking to go with it. He caught her arm to stop her from walking away. "There was a time when you would have servants serve us tea. Why now do you serve it to me? Elgan left you a manor, servants, money, he must have! Drop the charade Lorelyn, why do you hide who you are?"

"Why not?" Her voice cracked, "Without him, I am nothing. This was the only life I ever knew before he came to me that winter. It is my home." She did not continue, and Carn could see the tears begin to well up in her eyes. He let his grip on her arm loosen so that his hand could slide down to meet hers, giving her comfort.

"He was my best friend, I should have been there for his family. I looked for you in Eldonar, but the manor house was abandoned, and no one knew your whereabouts. Then I was too late for you, too late for Aylan. Have you ever even told her about her past?" He accused gently.

Uncomfortable, she attempted to laugh it off using the joke Aylan often used herself: "No one ever accused her of being a lady!"

Carn's steady blue gaze never wavered, and he pushed on "You made sure of that, I know, but why? The silence lengthened between them, and as he became surer that no answer would follow, he delivered the words he knew she would detest: "I must ask you to accompany me to the castle, Duchess, your presence has been requested by the queen."

←———

Chapter 5
~ A Glimpse of a Lady ~

Carn and Lorelyn approached the castle together, with his horse in tow. He had insisted that he walk and she take the saddle, however she wouldn't hear of it. The best he could do was refuse to ride himself, so they walked congenially, shoulder to shoulder as the sun sank lower in the sky. At the same time Oslan was escorting Aylan back to the keep for the night. He had not told her that Carn had gone to see her mother, so it would be a surprise if she had seen them coming up the lane. Oslan and Carn had decided that since secrets held from the throne were involved, and the reaction of both family members were key to finding out the truth, they did not want to give mother and daughter a chance to talk about the situation before being brought before Queen Elsa. Luckily for Oslan and Carn's plan, Aylan did not see her mother, and Oslan walked more briskly, so they could keep a good distance ahead. Carn did his part by pausing long enough to hand his horse off to a stable boy with instructions to water and feed his stallion. Carn also ordered Lorelyn's things to be untied from the horse and placed in her room before they proceeded to the keep's front doors where Oslan and his companion had disappeared only moments before.

Travelling ahead of Carn and Lorelyn with Aylan now, as the older couple gained the foyer of the keep, Oslan lowered his voice to speak privately with Aylan. He fervently willed that she would do the same so the sound of her voice would not give them away as they began to ascend the stairs to the upper corridor. *Hopefully,* thought Oslan, *with her hair done up and wearing this gown, Aylan's own mother will not recognize her.* Seeing the couple walking together up ahead, with the girl's hand resting gently on Oslan's proffered arm, Lorelyn spoke to Carn in low tones. "Is this the prince's new fiancée? If so, then the rumours I have heard are certainly false."

"Rumours?" asked Carn casually with a sideways glance at Lorelyn. He stopped and turned to face her, giving Oslan a chance to lengthen the distance between them.

"Aye, I've been away. I left right after the first day of the tournament, and just got back yesterday. Riding through the towns on the way home, I heard scandalous stories of the prince becoming engaged to a common girl. I can see now though that they were just rumours, it is obviously not the case."

"You can't always believe what you hear, Milady." Carn responded casually. She shot him a look tinged with impatience, but kept it from her voice when she spoke. "Well I do hope I get a chance to see her up close," said Lorelyn, gushing slightly, "It's not every day that the kingdom's only prince and heir to the throne chooses a bride!" Oslan and Aylan disappeared into a hall upstairs, and Carn began walking once more.

"You will get your chance to see her tomorrow. You are to breakfast with the royal family, and Oslan's lady will be there too," Carn assured her.

"Aylan lives in the castle, and I bet she knows something of the girl." Lorelyn realized, "I must ask Aylan all about her."

"I must admit, she knows the prince's fiancée better than anyone." Carn offered as they finished mounting the staircase, and turned down a hall in the opposite direction of the wing housing Aylan's room. "But that too will have to wait," continued Carn, "For it is getting late tonight, and a servant will come to rouse you early for your breakfast with the Queen." They stopped outside a room and Carn opened it, allowing the door to swing in. He took up her hand with practiced ease, and bent low over it. His thick wavy blonde hair dangled toward the floor, and she was conscious of his rough calloused palm as his lips deftly brushed the back of her knuckles. He rose with a warm "Sleep well, Duchess, I will see you on the morrow." Then he turned and briskly walked away, leaving her to consider his back as he departed. Entering the room, she realized that she had been brought to one of the guest quarters reserved for noble friends of Endalwynndale. Stepping inside, she closed the door behind her, and saw that her floor had a purple rug with intricate designs, a writing desk and chair, and a four poster bed with cascading fabric that matched the colours of the rug. A wardrobe stood at attention on one wall, and after confirming that it was empty, Lorelyn found her travelling bag, and placed it on the bed. She unfastened the leather straps and opened it to reveal a gown the likes of which Aylan had never seen. *Aylan might fall over dead if she sees me in this,* the duchess thought to herself. Her fine gowns were stored in a secret chest hidden under the floorboards of their cottage's little bedroom. Aylan had never questioned why there were wooden floors only in the bedroom when the rest of the cottage was much more rustic. *All the better,* Lorelyn reflected, *it has allowed me to keep my secret, until now.* She placed her gown in the wardrobe, washed her face and hands after her afternoon trek, and put herself to bed being too nervous to eat. She sailed off into a fitful sleep, to dreams of her lost husband, of Carn...and of the queen.

←————

Chapter 6
~The Art of an Artifact~

As his servant opened the shutters, letting the cold morning light pierce through the openings in his bed's curtains, Oslan squeezed his eyes shut and groaned. He stretched, relishing the feeling of all his muscles growing taught and then comfortably loosening as he released each one. He arose, full of trepidation for the impending meal. As he padded to his chamber pot, he considered the upcoming breakfast, and hoped that it would not be a catastrophe. *This conversation will determine whether I marry for love, or if I am to be bound by my father's decree to have an arranged marriage to a stranger I may never grow to love,* Oslan thought scornfully. *How could I, when my heart already belongs to another?*

Ever since Oslan neared the age of thirteen, the common marrying age for boys in Endalwynndale, his father, King Eurilas, had shown a growing unease at the fact that Oslan seemed to have no inclination towards marrying any girl. The prince knew that the law stated that he could not ascend to the throne until he was wed, and Oslan had been in no hurry to do either. His father had still been young, and Oslan was in no rush to take the throne from him. He simply had not found a girl that was right for him. He had believed that he had all the time in the world to find his match. The assassination of the king had proved that he had been mistaken.

The kingdom now anxiously awaited its next king, and he planned to take on the position with Aylan as his queen. *If she will still have me after this,* Oslan thought dejectedly. *May brightness shine on me and let me be able to repair the damage that I am about to inflict.* He hoped in his heart of hearts that she would forgive his meddling in the happy life her mother had created for her. He prayed that she would come to understand why he had chosen to leave her in the dark when he had discovered her family secrets. More importantly, he hoped that she could find it within her to forgive the plot he had formed with Carn to publicly reveal those secrets to the queen.

Oslan was not happy about the alternative way many royals wed in order to extend his or her kingdom. He had always maintained that he would marry upon finding a girl that would make him laugh, would fill him with wonder, and with whom he would want to start a family. *It also wouldn't hurt,* he reflected, *for her to be pleasing to the eye.* For him, Aylan was that person. She was smart, strong, and funny, and more beautiful than a sunset over the water on a clear summer's eve. Even when she had been younger, dressed as a boy, and trying to hide her freckles behind her hair, he had still found her to be pretty. Her strong will made life anything but boring, and her knowledge of herbology and magic shrouded her in mystery for him. He was smitten, pure and simple. He wanted her to be his, and somehow by the powers that be, she wanted to have him as well. He was determined to make it so, and he would not give up easily.

He dressed in the royal blue velvet tunic that he knew Aylan loved, and did something he almost never did: he decided that today he would don a crown. Oslan left his chambers, closing the door quietly behind him, and walked down the corridor to the North-East tower. The stairs going up would lead to the mews that housed his family's falcons. His plan instead took him downstairs toward the room at the base of the tower that contained the royal vault. As he descended into the dank cooler air, his arms broke out in goose bumps at the change in temperature. His eyes strained to see in the dimmer light of the torches ensconced on the walls. The knights standing on guard at intervals along the landings gave him the kingdom's salute, which he returned. The clatter of their armour echoed off the stone walls and stairs, spreading the news to the guards farther on that someone was coming.

His footfalls resonated with him, and the muffled sounds of alert voices, scraping chairs, and clanging armour met his ears as he rounded the last stair case. When he gained the basement floor, he could tell that the knights stationed in front of the heavy iron doors had just straightened from a card game. Hands of the cards were still fanned on the table, and one chair had spilled to the floor, presumably with the owner's hasty retreat from the hand.

The prince lifted an eyebrow at the sight of the purse of coppers on the table, and the small pile gathered in front of each man's place. He could see the surprise on their faces to see him, and one of them cleared his throat to draw his attention away from the sight of their frowned upon pass-time. He waved it off, aware that he had caught them by surprise, and equally aware that this must be one of the most secure and boring posts to serve on. An enemy would first have to penetrate the castle walls, gain entry past the knights at the entrance to the keep, and then get by the hundreds of knights and knights-in-training in order to even gain the staircase. These men would by then have had much warning that folly was upon them, allowing them to get neatly into position in case of an emergency.

Perhaps, he chuckled to himself, *I should come down here regularly, just to spook them into action a little more often.* He frowned at their gambling, but tucked away the fact that at least his knights were being paid well enough to do so. As he usually chose to go bareheaded, he had not been here for a long time. In fact, he had not returned since he was surprised by the king one day, who thought to nudge him closer to marriage by showing him his future inheritance. Many a month had passed since then, and this was his first trip to the vault on his own.

He approached the doors, and removed the heavy key which lay on a chain around his neck in preparation for this visit. He heard the audible clacks of the key turning in the vault's lock, and the guards hefted open the double doors, whose metal hinges squealed and echoed off the stone walls. One knight handed the prince a torch from a sconce on the wall, and as he entered, the gleam and glitter of gold reflected the dancing fire light again and again. The vault had compartments built into its walls that were all but brimming with piles of gold, and smaller piles of silver. There were rings, necklaces, intricate hair combs, broaches and bracelets. It contained the combined wealth of all of the kings, queens, princes and princesses of Endalwynndale that had come before him.

He placed the torch into one of the vault's sconces, and walked to the centre table. Only the sound of grit under his shoes and his shaky breath accompanied him. The table was covered in an array of brightly coloured velvet pillows, upon which sat the crown jewels. A succession of awe-inspiring crowns, tiaras, and circlets gleamed up at him in the fire light. They were all different sizes, contained jewels of varying colours, and were forged from a range of metals. The one he chose now was technically his, though only recently had this become the case. He lifted the crown that had belonged to his father around the time of his own coronation. It was heavy, made of a wide band of gold and rimmed with a cushion of navy blue velvet around the base. The centre front peak was decorated with a blue diamond as big as Oslan's flawless amber-green eyes. This was flanked by rubies in the next two points, followed by emeralds in the next. Garnets and onyx finished the design around the back, in succession growing smaller and smaller. He looked at his reflection briefly in the shiny surface of the diamond, and lifted the crown reverently to his head.

Oslan felt the weight of his father's crown and it sobered him. It was as if he carried the burden of the situation with him. He turned, holding his head up high. He retrieved the torch from the wall and passed by his knights, bidding them shut the doors behind him so he could re-lock the vault. He turned to one of the older men he knew personally from the training field, and asked unsteadily, "How do I look?"

"By the shields, Sire," the knight exclaimed, "you look like the spitting image of your father just after his coronation!"

"Excellent." The prince replied grimly. *Forgive me Mother,* he thought as he started back up the stairs toward the impending breakfast in the great room, *but I need all the leverage I can get, and Aylan and her mother are not the only ones that deserve to be appraised of my situation. I just hope this shock does your heart no lasting harm.*

← ———————

Chapter 7
~ Reservations ~

In the grand room, the regal queen was already seated, wearing what she had come to think of as her power crown. Dressed in a gown of red and gold, she waited patiently, poised with head held high. She was flanked by two serving girls standing behind her, each within a pace of her chair at the head of the table. The seats at the queen's right hand sat empty, held in reserve for her son and guest. On her left sat her three daughters, Oslan's sisters, in a succession of younger spitting images of the queen. The oldest princess, Talithan, with her hair pinned up in the fashion of their mother, was older than Oslan by a couple of years and fewer months. She was almost considered a spinster at this unmarried age. Although she had been wooed by an unmatched number of men, she had smartly turned each one down, owing to distasteful habits, poor hygiene, and on one occasion, simply on account of his bad breath. Oslan believed that she longed for a life in the country away from the castle, and was waiting for him to take the throne so he would change the law to state that she could marry a countryman. On this morning, she wore a dress of light crystal blue that many of her suitors had admired and many a lady had envied.

The only one with amber-green eyes to match her brother's, was Tanyan, Oslan's middle and closest sister. She was born in the same year as Oslan, though only just, making her eleven months his senior. Sitting farthest from the queen, her hair was in its customary curly dark cascade down her back, and she was sporting a dress of soft yellow that was quite modest for her age. She had been content with an arranged marriage, and had been betrothed when she had first come of marrying age. However, her intended had grown seriously ill during the winter months of that year, and had passed on as surely as the king had. She often dressed younger since their father died, refusing to be wooed by anyone out of respect for the customary three months of mourning following their father's early demise. Now that the year had passed since her first loss, and the respectful three months for her father were also up, she bided her time patiently to court again. She loved her brother dearly, and knowing that the first royal wedding of this generation would be a grand event indeed, she chose to wait so as not to overshadow her brother's exchange of vows and rise to the throne.

Trindalynn, the somewhat spoiled youngest member of the family had yet to have her eighth birthday. Coming a full five years and some months after the queen had believed her child bearing years to be at an end, Trindalynn's birth seemed to have almost come as an afterthought. Her chestnut locks now fell around her angelic face in short curls, and she wore an amethyst coloured dress trimmed with white lace that she was quite fond of. Her pout and the set of her arms crossed over her chest displayed the impatience she felt at having to wait to dine on the arrival of the rest of their guests. Not yet able to reach the floor, her tiny feet kicked at the air, swinging to and fro under the table in annoyance.

A servant dressed in the men's typical castle livery consisting of black leggings and grey-brown tunic, came through the entryway of the great room and held the door open as Lorelyn entered. She whispered briefly in his ear as she passed, and he announced: "Presenting the honorable Lorelyn Suresword, Duchess of Eldonar," before removing himself from the room and shutting the door behind him. The queen beheld the curtseying Lorelyn, in an elegant white dress, with her hair bound within an intricate pearl-studded caul. Queen Elsa motioned to the seats on her right.

"Come sit by me," she invited, "we have much to discuss."

Lorelyn took her place in the seat of honour, and the queen motioned for the servants to begin pouring their morning's watered wine. No sooner had the last drop of wine fallen into the pool within the last cup, when Trindalynn scooped hers up off the table and started to gulp it down. She froze under the sharp gaze of Elsa, whose attention was drawn away from Lorelyn at the sound of her youngest daughter's wet *slurp*.

Embarrassed at having not behaved as a princess should, Trindalynn immediately replaced her cup, daintily daubed at the edges of her mouth with her napkin, and folded her hands in her lap, head bowed. The queen once again focused on Lorelyn, thinking of her entrance. "I see you have decided to come to your senses," Elsa began, but before Lorelyn could respond or the queen continue with her lecture, the door opened a second time.

The servant entered once again, held the door and announced: "presenting Aylan Suresword." Lorelyn adjusted her position to see her daughter enter. Aylan came in wearing a stunning deep green dress made from a light loose fitting fabric. It had long sleeves, a fitted top with a rounded low neckline and a high waist. The skirts showed three layers of different lengths, which were all green, and each a shade darker than the last. Her now long blonde hair was not pulled up, but was braided smoothly down her back to just below her shoulder blades. Her mother sat agape, having not seen her now adult child in anything but a tunic since she had started to dress herself.

"Come sit by me!" Tanyan begged her, having not spent a great deal of time with Aylan since the announcement of her engagement at the ball. Aylan moved into the room, finally allowing Millie, her appointed lady-in-waiting to enter the room after her. Millie trailed after her to the table, and took up a position against the wall between two guards. Aylan accepted the offered seat, which put her in a position to speak with the prince when he sat across the table, but which was still close enough to the queen that everyone at the table would hear any conversation that took place. She sat and was greeted by Tanyan with a brief kiss on the cheek under the gaze of the queen. Millie poked the servant with the wine and berated him in a hoarse whisper "Well what are you waiting for? Milady is thirsty and her chalice is yet dry!" The agitated servant tried to step forward, but Millie smartly plucked the pitcher from the maid's hands and moved quickly to fill the empty goblet herself. As she poured, Aylan leaned over to whisper in her ear: "It's not like Oslan to let me beat him to breakfast, and why is that courtier gaping at me like a fish? Millie drew her attention away from the wine long enough to snatch a glance at Lorelyn, at which point her hand faltered and wine sloshed onto the table.

"Aylan, it's your mother!" Millie gasped, flustered.

"Careful you fool!" bellowed the queen, already irritable that her son was late, when it had been he who had arranged this meeting. Another servant stepped up to wipe the table clean, but was waved away. "Just go get the meal!" Elsa ordered in a tired voice.

Then Aylan truly took the time to notice the

woman in the white dress seated on the other side of table. "Mother, what are you doing here," Aylan asked, astounded, "and wherever did you get that dress?"   Lorelyn felt self-conscious with her daughter's eyes on her, looking at her as if she was some kind of new interesting flower she could mash into a potion.

The queen began to respond, "Your mother-", but was cut off by Oslan who had entered without being introduced, and who continued without skipping a beat: "Will explain all that to you in due time." Then, seeing the expression on Queen Elsa's face, as if she were seeing a ghost, he went on, "Right after we enjoy a nice family meal together."

Tanyan looked at her brother, a huge grin spreading across her face. She looked to the floundering queen, back to Oslan, and once more to her mother. Then to break the silence, she proclaimed "I would like the salt!" The exclamation brought everyone back from their reveries and the meal was begun.

$\longleftarrow$

Chapter 8
~The Lady of Eldonar~

Queen Elsa still sat stunned, not just at the interruption, but at the sight of her son. He looked every bit the king in his father's old crown. Oslan saw her visibly shake it off and eye him as she took her first sips of the recently refilled watered wine. He ignored the spot that was set for him beside Lorelyn to the queen's right, the place of an obedient son. Instead, he took a seat at the opposite end of the table from her, making it a new position of authority. Not only did this set the tone for the upcoming conversation, it also placed him in the seat closest to Aylan, so he could show her support and solidarity in what was about to come. Now that the whole royal family was present, the servants began to bring out the mild repast of trenchers of toast and salmon. As food was placed in front of the princesses, his youngest sister Trindalynn blurted out: "You look rather like Daddy. Are you going to be king now?"

Everyone at the table glanced quickly at the queen as she fumbled her goblet back onto the table. "That remains to be seen, Dear." she said coolly, recovering herself while glaring at Oslan.

Lorelyn chose this time to speak up, "If it pleases her majesty," she began, "the rumours across the land are that Oslan has become engaged. Is it not just a matter of the wedding then till he does become king?"

"Yes, he must first marry," Elsa replied, "but it remains to be seen whether he has chosen an appropriate bride."

"I had heard that he had chosen a peasant. However, I saw his intended from afar last night, and she seems truly to hold herself as a noble." Lorelyn confided, "It seems obvious that the rumours were untrue." She finished as she took a bite of toast with fish.

"A pretty dress does not a noble make." The queen responded firmly. "The question is about her pedigree, not her looks!"

Oslan looked pointedly at Aylan, and gave his head an imperceptible shake meant only for her, *don't react, just listen.* She gave him a curt nod, showing him that she would hold her peace...for now. She followed this up with taking her own bite of the morning meal so as not to be able to break the silence with her voice.

Now Oslan turned toward Lorelyn, and took a deep breath to steady his nerves. He was ready to seize the moment, and risking all on Aylan's mother's response, let the cat out of the bag. "Madam, I have fallen quite madly for your daughter. It is her I mean to marry." As he spoke, he held his hand openly toward Aylan, who deftly slipped her fingers into his grasp over the table. Feeling a surge of reassurance, he went on: "The only thing that now stands between the throne, happiness and myself, is the truth. Please explain to my mother, the queen, that I have not in fact become engaged to a common girl." He implored.

Lorelyn began to slowly shake her head back and forth in denial. "Aylan, Your Majesty," Lorelyn faltered, unsure of how to begin. Finally, she seemed to pull herself up by the bootstraps and was able to go on. She decided on looking to the queen as she spoke, but Oslan got the feeling that it was really Aylan she was addressing. "And to think," she finally said ironically, "that the whole pretence was to prevent her from a marriage to a lord, and she goes and gets engaged to a prince!"

"What pretence mother?" Aylan exclaimed,

"And why should you be afraid of me marrying a lord of all people? I am but a farm girl, why should any lord want me?"

"Indeed," added the queen, who was prevented from saying more by the fierce look Oslan shot her way. He was grimly determined not to let his mother ruin this moment for Aylan, no matter how much she tried to interfere. He felt that Aylan deserved to know that things were not as they seemed. Of everything about her life that she had up until now believed to be true, there were some parts that had been kept secret from her, and were now of some import. He was only sorry that this had to happen in front of his family, but it was necessary. He knew that if Aylan were to have been allowed this private moment with her own mother, then came to tell the queen, he could see how the Queen might think it was yet another scheme they had cooked up to allow the two of them to be together.

"Aylan, "Lorelyn continued, now looking at her daughter, "you were just an infant when your father died. You knew your father as Elgan Suresword, king's knight. I'm not sorry that I led you to believe this, it was for your own protection."

"Pish tosh!" the queen interjected, "That's ridiculous, a noble needs no protection from other lords, she would have had all the protection she needed with the knights under your command!"

"Mother," Oslan roared, "I think my *fiancée* deserves to hear the whole story from her own mother's lips, without interruption or interference from you."

Queen Elsa paled visibly and was silenced. Startled, Aylan turned to the prince. "You knew about this?"

"Only since last night, I swear it. Even then, I

wasn't completely sure. This is my confirmation as it is yours. I brought you and your mother together today so you could find out who you truly are." Then, regarding Lorelyn, he continued, "Please, do go on."

"You have to understand, I lived my whole life as a commoner. When my husband died, I simply went back to the only home I ever knew without him. I saw how lords and ladies act and treat each other. They seem to think they own the world, and sometimes their women besides." Lorelyn spoke directly to Aylan now. "You have to understand dear, a noble's life might be one of ease, but when I married your father, I had come from the humble roots you've lived most of your life in. He whisked me away to his manor and we were wed. It was like a fairy tale. He was more than a knight, but he was also a diamond in the rough, the exception to the rule.

Oslan sneaked a glance at Aylan to see how she faired. He could see her putting two and two together in her mind, the cogs turning.

Lorelyn continued, "He did not simply choose or claim me, Aylan, he met me, spoke to me, spent time with me, and we fell in love. That is almost unheard of in a noble's life. Most of the nobles I have met looked down their noses at ordinary folk, and that's who I had been, a common farm-girl. I did not think I could bare it if I raised you as the lady you are, and one day saw that same look of distain or disapproval on your face toward people like me. Commoners might be stuck living within meagre means that they can provide for themselves, but they have the luxury of living honestly, and can find love with whom they choose. They aren't bound to expand the manor they own or the people they preside over through marriage, which is usually the noble way of things. Your father showed me that there can be more to noble life than that. That is why I left, to escape the pretences others tried to presume upon his death. I did not want you to grow up knowing nothing of the people that work the land and make this country what it is.

"Mother, you're not making any sense, what do you mean my father was more than a knight? What manor do you speak of?" Aylan pressed.

Lorelyn took a deep steadying breath before answering. "Your aunt, the Countess of Eshenberg, did not earn her title through marriage. It was her birthright. Your father was the Duke of Eldonar, Aylan. I am the Duchess."

Oslan regarded the look of shock on his fiancée's face. "Aylan," he finished for her, "You are the Lady of Eldonar."

⇐————

Chapter 9
~ To Visit a Villain ~

The queen, placated, finally gave her consent for Oslan to marry Aylan. For her part, Lorelyn had spent hours after breakfast with her daughter filling in all the missing pieces of her life and her father's before her. Oslan later learned that since Aylan had been capable of handling the farm alone, she had been used to her mother's absences. According to Aylan, they were long trips that her mother would take to supposedly visit her aunt, the Countess. As it turned out though, Lorelyn had actually been travelling north to Eldonar to complete business that her station demanded. Aylan's mother had finally followed Queen Elsa's suit, and had also acquiesced to let the couple marry, but only after ascertaining that it was indeed what Aylan wanted. The wedding was set for the very next week, and Oslan was to be coronated within the space of a month.

Oslan made his way to the South-West tower, the one that housed the dungeons underground, and Zaltreous' cell in the tower high above. Taking the grey stone steps two at a time up and around the winding staircase, Oslan's red tunic flashed with natural light every time he passed an arrow slit in the outer wall. With the matter of the wedding having been settled the day before, his focus today had turned back to his captive high above the keep.

Zaltreous was the evil mage that had threatened to capture Endalwynndale in his hatred for King Eurilas' former mage, Lazelan. The rejection of the love of Lazelan's woman had sparked this hatred for the good mage, his former friend. Enraged, Zaltreous had turned to an evil book of magic called the *Almatraek Dim*, which Carn had searched for, and had been thought lost at sea for years.   Now that it had resurfaced, Oslan intended to try to get as much information out of Zaltreous as he could in the hopes of finding its sister book, the *Almatraek Bright.* This second book had been created by good mages to thwart the spells in the *Almatraek Dim,* and it held many antidotes and counter-spells that only existed within its pages.   Oslan didn't know how willing Zaltreous would be to talk, or if he would have any knowledge about the other book of magic.   The prince didn't mind using extra pressure to find out what he needed at this point.   Normally he would never condone such a thing, but it had been Zaltreous that had caused the death of Oslan's father, the king.

Oslan came around the last bend of the staircase, revealing two guards in cloaks with their backs to the doors.   The cloaks had been designed specially by Lazelan before he had started his journey back to his own land, Ethik.   The cloaks were black and fell all the way to the floor, leaving not even their ankles or boots exposed.   With the hoods up to protect the guards' necks and heads, the   kingdom's   embroidered   emblem,   the   fire breathing dragon, was visible on the back.   Lazelan had cast a spell on each of the cloaks to shield them from magic.   It was just an extra precaution, but Oslan had insisted, since he had seen the scope of possibilities when it came to Zaltreous and his spells.   Zaltreous' cell had been doctored from its usual state to prevent him from casting.   Aylan had created   little   pouches   of   herbs   that   would continually zap just enough of Zaltreous' energy to preclude him from building up an energy pool large enough to cast even the smallest spell.   These packets had been bricked right into the walls so that the prisoner could not interfere with them.   He had been induced into a deep sleep by magic upon arriving in Endalwynndale before he was removed from the brig of the boat on which he was being transported. Then he was left in the cell for the packets to take effect. The slumber spell had been lifted, and he had been stuck there ever since.

Oslan's guards saluted him, but did not stand aside to allow him access to the door. "Carn will be here in moments to go in with you, Your Highness." One guard informed him gruffly. "He ordered us to ask you to wait for him before entering. He said it's for your own safety." He added apologetically. No sooner had the words left the guard's mouth then Oslan heard Carn's armour clanking as he ascended the stairs to meet the prince. *Everyone seems anxious to have me on the throne as king, yet they all act as if they know better than me,* the prince grumbled. *I wish they would make up their minds, and trust my decisions. This type of situation is so awkward and frustrating. Soon it will only be a matter of exerting my power as king, though I do wish they would learn that I know what is best for my own kingdom.*

"Sire," Carn addressed him.

"Carn," Oslan said stiffly back, his look of frustration catching Carn's eye. The prince knew that Carn had seen it, and he was glad. *Maybe it will make him think twice before ordering my own guards to stop me. I'm not a fragile babe anymore.*

Now the guards stood aside looking relieved that the prince had not said anything to contradict their orders. That would have been an unpleasant situation to have to deal with. The guard that had not spoken unhooked the large key ring at his belt. There were keys on the circlet of iron for every door in the dungeon at the bottom of the tower, including a smaller key to the door up here. The guard deftly unlocked the door and stood aside, letting Carn draw his sword and open the door for himself. With his hand on the handle, Carn glanced back to the prince, who nodded that he was ready.

*   *   *

Inside the dim cell, Zaltreous, stooped and facing the wall, felt the chill of a cold sweat of fear as he heard the approaching footsteps outside. At the sound of the guard's voice just on the other side of the door, talking to the prince, Zaltreous' heart leapt into his mouth. He looked around frantically, searching for a way to clean up the mess without being discovered. The hand holding the fork began to shake in fear. *This could ruin everything!* he thought desperately. He had been feverishly using the butt-end of the fork to chisel away the mortar between the bricks, and now had a sizeable pile of dust and rubble at his feet. He quickly wiped the fork off on his bed and replaced it on his breakfast tray. His sleeping cot was pulled out from the wall where he had been digging, but there was no time to move it back as the door swung opened. He knew he had only precious moments as the door shed light on his much dimmer room, before the prince's eyes would adjust and the sight before him would reveal all. Zaltreous moved fast, rounding the bed, he hastily hid his hands behind his back, and used the backs of his legs to push the bed roughly against the wall as the prince and his man entered. The cot came to rest over the pile of rubble, blocking the spot on the wall where he had been digging.

*   *   *

Oslan watched as the door swung inward, revealing a dark room beyond. The two armed men,

Oslan now fifteen, and Carn thirty-three, waited for their eyes to adjust and warily entered the dim cell before them. The room contained a simple bed, a desk, chair, a stinking chamber pot, and a single candle that was replaced every time it burned down. The only window had been bricked in upon Zaltreous' arrival, to prevent him from being able to steal the energy from passers-by in the square below.

"Welcome, my esteemed guests." The reedy voice said from the shadows. The lack of natural light did little for Zaltreous' complexion, and his face swam to them, ghostly white under his shock of lanky black hair in the gloom of the small jail. Once handsome, now the deep dark circles of restless nights under his eyes marred his good looks.

"You sound parched," commented Carn, "I think we can all do with a cool mug of water."

"You are too gracious, Sir Carn," Zaltreous replied, his calculating eyes shining. "And you," he continued, addressing the prince with a shallow bow, "I am honoured to be visited by the-" he paused, looking for a crown, but seeing only Oslan's bare head, continued, "future king." He finished.

Vehemently, in the prince's mind he screamed back: *There would be no need for a future king if-* the prince stopped himself in mid-thought. *It is said that it is easier to catch a fly with honey than vinegar. As much as I dislike this knave, I need information from him. If I am able to get it out of him with sweetness, I must.* He acknowledged the bow with a nod of the head. Out loud, he replied "Yes, that is to be remedied soon." Oslan noticed fine beads of sweat perching on Zaltreous' forehead just below the slicked back hairline. "I trust it doesn't get too hot in here during the day?" He inquired.

"The sun doesn't really have a chance to warm my room, Sire." Zaltreous told him while shifting his weight uncomfortably from one foot to the other. After an awkward moment, Oslan pressed on.

"We have some questions for you about the *Almatraek Dim* and the *Almatraek Bright.*"

Zaltreous' eyes glistened in the candle light as he looked from the crown prince to Carn and back again. Carn stood relaxed, but with his sword still in hand. "What do you wish to know?" Zaltreous hedged while stepping away from his bed. He tripped, causing him to stumble into Carn, who caught him and helped him back to his feet.

"Please forgive me," Zaltreous simpered as he righted himself, now appearing to stand taller. "I find it easy to stumble when the light is so dim." He seemed to curse under his breath at his clumsiness, but it was too low for the prince to hear. Almost as if to prove his point, the candle light flickered and dimmed slightly if only for a split second.

⇐———

Chapter 10
~ History or His Story ~

The water had come and the tankards drained. Hours of talk passed in the small room. The prince intermittently shivered or felt sweat spring up on his brow as the temperature in the small cell seemed to change with the weather outside. Though the brickwork was thick and no sun could penetrate into the darkness from outside, the temperature rose, or cooled considerably with what must have been the heat from the sun and cold wind outside coming through the brickwork.

Surprisingly, Zaltreous had talked freely. He told Oslan of how the book had come into his possession while he had been training at the docks to move water with magic. Standing on the grassy shoreline at the land end of a dock, he had been pushing a toy sailboat around by manipulating the size of the waves around it. He began creating bigger and bigger waves, finally sinking the tiny boat when one crashed over its deck, crushing its small sails. His toy now destroyed, he contemplated sending even bigger waves toward the real boats tethered at the dock. *I can do it too,* he thought smugly. *Those fools at the university have no idea what I'm already capable of. Not that I'll ever tell them. If they ever found out how much I can really do, they'd likely try to poke or prod me to find out why I'm different from my classmates. Or worse, some professor with a big ambition might try to use me for their lackey.*

He began putting more and more force into the ocean, creating more powerful whitecaps that would be able to toss even a full sized vessel. He brought the waves in toward the shore. They splashed over his feet and legs, but he did not move, too captivated by his magical ability. Looking farther and farther out over the water he noticed a solid object ride the crest of a large wave, totter on the brink for a split second, and then plunge under the cold spray. He thought that would be it, whatever it was had most surely been ruined as his boat had been. However, an instant later it floated up again, breaking the ocean's surface with a buffer of space much larger than the object appeared to warrant. Intrigued, he let his other waves die, and focused all of his energy on the water around the floating item. He had used wave after wave to push it close enough to the shore for him to wade out and collect it.

Atop rough-hewn broken boards, a small makeshift raft made of some planks, laid a very large, leather bound tome. Held shut with two leather straps buckled over its cover, it was bone dry despite its swim in the drink. He reached for it and felt his hands bump into an invisible barrier. *Magic!* He realized. *Whoever set it adrift must have protected it from the elements and the ocean. Perhaps it might be worth something,* he mused excitedly. He managed to get his hands under the planks and lifted them and the book both together. With a glance around to make sure no one had noticed what he was doing, he carried his load to a space behind a nearby bush, away from prying eyes. Setting it down on the ground, he felt for his reservoir of magical energy. He brought some out of his core and focussed it through his hands onto the invisible dome that seemed connected to the planks. Bringing to mind the words in Almatrae, the ancient language that all magic was cast from, he formed his spell: "Krant uti inktal," *Break this spell.* The dome seemed to glow a light purple only for a moment, then turned invisible once more. Cutting off the flow of energy, Zaltreous went for the book. Again, his hands bumped into the barrier. *That should have worked!* He thought, frustrated. *No matter, there are others spells that yet might free the book.* He focussed his energy once again at his mark. "Sauxinktal uti gienla," *Dispel this magic,* he commanded. Still, the barrier resisted. *Perhaps there is a stronger incantation yet unknown to me,* he reasoned. Leaving his broken toy boat behind, he collected his other things and walked quickly with his new treasure back to his room at the university where he would be able to get a better look at what he had found.

Oslan and Carn listened to Zaltreous speak for a long time. When they were satisfied with the new information they had collected, they left the mage locked safely in his cell, and went to seek out the prince's seer. They walked through the palace corridors, past tapestries depicting the kingdom's past battles, to her quarters. They had no sooner approached her room and the prince knocked politely on her door, when it came flying open.

"What has happened to Aylan?" Sasha burst frantically into their faces. Deeply alarmed, Oslan demanded she speak. "I have not seen Aylan today. We came from visiting Zaltreous. What harm has taken place, Sasha?"

"Maybe nothing," she replied, "was Carn with you the whole time you remained in the tower?"

"I haven't left the prince's side in hours." Carn confirmed. Sasha seemed visibly relieved at that, and asked them inside. Sasha's room, more lavish than most guests' in the castle, had an anti-chamber like the prince's. It was there that the three sat on sturdy wooden chairs, each covered by a cushion for comfort. The chairs were arranged around a low table over a worn blue and gold carpet that had been brought to this room when Tanyan, Oslan's oldest sister, had had a new one made for her own room. Off to the side, stood a writing desk with a mirror above it and a bench seat pushed underneath.

"I knew you were coming, and took the liberty of having water boiled for us. It should arrive at any moment." Sasha confided.

"What did you witness between Carn and my soon-to-be wife?" Oslan asked, unsettled still because of Sasha's outburst.

"I wasn't sure if it was something that had happened, or something yet to come," Sasha explained, "I only saw Carn approach Aylan, and her collapse. Carn's body blocked my view of why."

Carn and Oslan exchanged an uneasy glance. "I would never harm Aylan, Your Majesty," the knight professed.

"I know you wouldn't, Carn. I just wish I knew more details of what was to happen." The prince reassured him.

"It frustrates me as it does you." Sasha divulged, "Though it is a useful gift, it is an uncertain one. Things do not often change once I have seen them, though sometimes they come to pass in a way I had not anticipated."

"I shall be extra careful whenever I am around her, Sire." Carn concluded, "No harm will befall her because of me."

The prince only nodded, for before he could speak, a knock sounded at the door, followed by a muffled "Hot water, Milady!"

Sasha rose and crossed the room to admit the servant, who brought in a steaming covered jug of hot water and set it on the low table. Sasha thanked the servant who then left them to their conversation. She crossed the room to her dressing table, and opened a drawer, extracting a small leather pouch that Oslan recognized as belonging to Aylan. Sasha returned to the sitting area while opening the pouch, and carefully removed a pinch of the sweet smelling dried leaves from inside. Carn helpfully removed the lid of the jug, and Sasha was able to add the mixture to the water. "This will make a most delicious tisane, good for revitalizing the mind, Aylan assures me."

Carn replaced the lid to allow the leaves to transform the water into a strongly brewed tea. The men talked about their meeting with Zaltreous, and asked her if she had learned anything about the dangerous book within their walls.

Chapter 11
~Dreaming and Scheming~

Sasha confirmed what the men had heard. Her light brown eyes touched on Oslan then rested on Carn as she revealed what she had learned, looking for verification herself. At Oslan's request, she had visited the *Almatraek Dim* where it was locked away and guarded. Being in its presence made her uneasy, for within its pages were incantations of torture, theft, possession and death. Aylan had told her that there were recipes for poisons and draughts that could incapacitate a man, kill him, or force him to transform. Though the book had no power on its own, in the wrong hands, it could be a lethal weapon. When it had been in Zaltreous' possession, he had been successful in killing the king, and had almost single-handedly taken over this very kingdom.

Inwardly she shuttered, remembering what she had seen. She had returned to her room to put herself into a deeper trance, allowing her vision to pull her toward the book and it's past. She told them that it had taken Zaltreous months before learning an incantation to break the spell over the book. It had been shielded, and it took a spell to specifically break the shield in order to set the book free. He had opened it, read the inscription, and been afraid of its contents enough to hide it for the next two years of his training. It wasn't until after he had surpassed his professors and had become sure that there was nothing else to learn, that he even remembered the book. Still, he had not ventured to even leaf through its pages.

Then there was the fateful night that Lazelan's fiancée had turned Zaltreous down, sending him into a blind rage. He had returned to its hiding spot, and it was then that he searched through the book in earnest, in order to bring Lazelan down. Oslan and Carn knew the rest of that story, as they had lived it. But Zaltreous had not been the book's first or even second owner. There had been countless mages that had used the tome for no good, and had added to it to make it stronger.

It had been the prior keeper of the *Almatraek Dim*, the one that had set it adrift for the next dark mage to find, that had killed Elgan Suresword, Duke of Eldonar, so many years ago. Carn, Elgan, and some other knights of King Eurilas' had gone on Ormond's orders to try to capture the book and destroy it. The king's general, Ormond, was respected and always obeyed despite the months the mission would take the knights away from their families.

Sasha paused in her telling in order to pour tea for the three of them. She sat, rearranging her golden silk dress, took a moment to collect her thoughts, and went on.

The previous keeper of the *Almatraek Dim* had used the book to acquire riches, land and power, and had become a lord, making it harder for the knights to gain access to him without being noticed. To their advantage, they found that the mage lord, a man by the name of Meltrabus, had been planning a trip on a boat across the Ocean of Empathy. They hired their own craft and followed in hot pursuit, knowing the book would be on board. After two days of travelling and breathing the salty air, they caught up to the lord who had tried to outrun them. Their ship was by far a faster vessel, which cut through the water as if it was flying. The mage sent a spell into the clouds to try to slow them, but to no avail, for the tossing of the sea had made him sick, and he had not been able to concentrate long enough to make the spell stick. The heroes soon drew abreast of the smaller ship.

The knights attempted to board it, and in the clash of swords and blows with the crew of the other ship who tried to defend their decks, Elgan had been hit with a paralyzing spell to which they had no antidote. There he had remained for a split second teetering on the railing, one foot raised in mid stride as he had prepared to leap from one boat to the other. The ships collided, jilting him. His sword and shield toppled from his frozen hands, clattering to the ship's deck. Unable to move to save himself, he tumbled off the railing and into the depths of the ocean below. With the weight of his armour, he sunk swiftly below the cold waves, too quickly to be saved. In the rain, Carn had heroically made ready to dive into the water after him, but was held on board by two other knights, who pulled him out of the way of another blast of magic that narrowly missed him.

The wind from his own storm threw the mage's tiny vessel around, and Eurilas' men only just managed to scramble back to their own bigger ship before the other was capsized by a huge wave. Lightning struck the smaller boat, and everyone could hear its hull crack in two. Debris began to float away from the wreck, and the knights attempted to save anyone they could, taking them aboard their craft. They looked for Meltrabus, and after searching the waves for some time, the band finally gave up, taking for granted that the evil mage had perished. However, in his final moments of life, they missed seeing the mage cast his shield over his beloved book before he too sank below the surface.

The book had drifted for weeks. It had been dashed upon a stand of rocks and there it had rested under the blazing sun for the longest time until the same storm freed it once more that had torn Lazelan's boat in two all those years later.

"I remember that battle, Sire," Carn commented when Sasha had finished. "That was a dark day that took many good men, both ours and the innocent sailors that knew not what *Lord* Meltrabus was up to," Carn spat. "I would have given my life to return with that book for your father, and almost did. It cripples my countenance to think that it was saved. It would have been better for everyone if it had suffered a watery grave to match its master's."

"The important thing," Oslan reassured him, "is that we possess the book now. Worry not, my good friend. Thank you Sasha for your words, we shall meet again soon, I must-"

Sasha surprised them by interrupting him with a new topic. "Honestly, Sire, you're as bad as Aylan!" She griped. "The only thing you *must* do right now is to go see the tailor. He awaits you, Your Majesty, in order to talk to you about your garments for the wedding." At the mention of the wedding, her already musical voice seemed to rise in excitement. The prince raised an eyebrow at her, and started to object. "Carn and I have much to do."

Again he was cut off, this time by Carn who seemed to finish his sentence: "in order to get ready for your big day. I will make sure that the prince finds his way to the tailor right away Sasha, rest assured, he will have plenty of time to make the prince's clothes." Carn quietly chuckled deep down in his chest as Oslan threw up his hands in surrender.

Chapter 12
~ Bearing Arms ~

Carn and Oslan returned from seeing the tailor with the prince's head still spinning. He had never given much thought to his clothing in the past. He was usually measured, and his mother and sisters arranged the rest. It boggled his mind to learn about how many weights, designs and shades of fabric there were to choose from. Now he had a new appreciation for the countless hours that his sisters had spent with the little man that made all of their clothes.

After approaching a couple of servants to inquire as to the ladies' whereabouts, they learned that Sasha had gone to the gardens to try to pick flowers with Aylan for her bridal bouquet. The men found Sasha adding more flowers to the armful that Aylan stood holding on the path between the rose bushes. Millie was there too, and as Sasha added some blooms to the pile, the handmaid would remove others, changing their overall colour and shape.

Aylan stood patiently, absently blowing a renegade hair that had found its way out of her braid, up and out of her face. Oslan caught a glint of gold as it floated on her breath and shone in the sunlight. Sasha smiled to see the men approaching, and turned her back to pick a bright magenta flower from a nearby bush. Oslan too plucked a deep red rose, full and fragrant from the plant he passed, in order to present it to Aylan as they strolled up. Filled with joy at the sight of her, Oslan remarked to himself, *Perhaps she will wear this one in her hair and think of me today.* Aylan too beamed with happiness, and Oslan, still out of earshot, could see her lips move as she seemed to talk to the flowers in her arms. The whole bunch gently lifted into the air, floating there before her. She began manipulating her fingers, moving the blooms around in the air, gathering them in an attractive bouquet. Millie plucked a sprig of tiny yellow flowers off of the nearby stone bench, and threw them up into Aylan's mix. These were special, even recognized by the men. With yellow edged petals that brightened to orange as they swooped inward, they ended with a fierce red centre. They were the kingdom's national flower called dragon's breath, and they looked like many bright tiny flames dancing on their stems.

The men began to get a better look at the way that tiny yellow flowers had been arranged almost like a shooting star within the splash of other colourful blossoms. As the men drew nearer, Aylan's smile faltered, and she swooned. The flowers rained down to the ground, and a stem or two were crushed under her foot as she took a staggering step to steady herself. Carn and Oslan saw the sudden change that had come over her, and as Millie called her name, both men rushed to catch the prince's fiancée before she could fall. Oslan's own flower dropped from his hand, forgotten, in his last quick paces to Aylan's side. He snatched her deftly out of the air as she fell, and bade Millie clear the bench so he could sit with his intended.

"I'm fine, really," Aylan said weakly, "I don't know what has come over me." In the commotion of clattering sounds of the men's running armour, jingling chain mail, and scuffling feet on their journey to catch Aylan, Sasha had turned back from the bush to see the rest of the scene unfold. The prince now sat with his arms protectively around Aylan, and Carn knelt by their side, with his back blocking the sight just as in Sasha's vision. She turned on him angrily, shoving his armour clad shoulder roughly, yet ineffectually. "What did I tell you? What have you done to her?" She barked in a way that should have sounded rough, yet managed to still come out sounding musical. At the impact of her slender handed shove, he attempted to sidle sideways away from her, while bringing up his two hands in a sign of surrender.

"He has not touched me!" Aylan professed woozily from the bench as Carn's boot-heel caught on the corner of his cape, sending him to his hands and knees under the pull of the snagged fabric.

"That," the prince pointed out calmly, trying to diffuse the situation before it got worse, "is why I do not wear cape, nor cloak. They always get in the way."

"What are those?" Millie remarked as she regarded the fallen knight. "I didn't know you used magic, Sir Carn."

"He doesn't." Sasha attested, plucking some dirty looking packets out from under the side of his breastplate where they were now exposed by his fall.

"Give them to me." Aylan demanded so she could get a better look at them. Sasha made to hand them to her, but as Aylan's fingers brushed the fabric, she was only able to manage a weak "Those are mine," before fainting back in Oslan's arms.

"Not anymore!" Millie cried as she moved quickly, pulling the packets out of Sasha's grasp, so she could run with them as far from Aylan as she could get. She disappeared from the garden, taking them well out of the path Aylan would need to take to get to her rooms. As the packets left her, Aylan's colour visibly improved, and her forehead smoothed as her head lulled against the prince's shoulder. Stricken, Carn looked openly at his friend as he righted himself. "Please forgive me Oslan," He grieved, for once forgetting about formality in his sorrow, "I don't know where they came from. I hope she will be alright."

"We would never have seen them if you had not fallen my friend," Oslan observed, relieved that the stress on Aylan seemed to be lessening. He began gently patting her cheeks to try to bring her around, when a massive clatter burst from the knights' barracks. Running feet and the sound of swords being unsheathed caught their attention. All of Ormond's army seemed to be amassing in front of the keep's large central doors. Knights from across the grounds ran to join them. Alarmed, Carn found his feet and rose to see what the commotion was about.

"It looks like the royal guard has been called together," Carn relayed as he watched Ormond shouting out orders from the castle stairs to those gathered in front of him. Carn saw a familiar young archer, a boy a bit on the scrawny side that carried his father's large bow. This was Thornton, Thorn to his friends, and the brother of Aylan's handmaid.

"Thorn!" Carn hailed him with a commanding voice, waving the young knight over. The brown-haired youth caught sight of him and made his way over at a quick jog, arrows jostling in the quiver he wore on his back. "What has happened?" Carn enquired, noticing how wide eyed and frightened the boy appeared.

"It is the mage locked in the tower, Sir," he began. The prince straightened noticeably in shock as he listened intently.

"What about him?" Oslan demanded, fearing the worst. The worst it was.

"Well, it...it seems...that he has escaped, Sire." Thornton finally stammered.

"But how?" Oslan asked, not really expecting

an answer.

"The packets," Carn concluded, "the ones zapping his energy from the walls. He must have figured a way to get them out. When Zaltreous stumbled in the cell, he put his arms around me. He must have planted them in my armour then. My cape covered the spot, hiding them nicely. We took them right out of his cell for him, unnoticed."

Horrified, Oslan's face blanched. "He has magic again."

Oslan saw Thorn hesitate. "There's more, Sire," he managed, "That evil book of his is also gone."

Chapter 13
~A Fox on the Lamb~

"She's about to come to." Sasha said distractedly as she watched the knights gather. Carn watched Thorn go back to get his instructions, and strained to hear Ormond's address. Oslan was finally able to get Aylan to open her eyes, and kissed her forehead in relief when she did so. He looked down on her as she smiled up at him weakly.

"We cannot let the men see Aylan brought down. It will weaken their resolve if they learn of it and decide that Zaltreous has done this to her. Any man would be afraid to fight off a mage powerful enough to take down a foe without even encountering them.

"I will take her in," Sasha offered, "We will pretend that the heat and the ordeal of the wedding had become too much for her. Mage or no mage, many people still see the lady in her first." Then she looked at Aylan, "Can you stand and walk, do you think?"

Aylan sat up "I think so," she mumbled groggily. She stood a bit unsteadily, but was able to cross the garden with the support of Sasha's arm. The two ladies made it into the castle without attracting the notice of the knights that were gathered by the doors. Instead of joining the throng of armour clad men at the back, Oslan and Carn walked around to stand next to Ormond, Oslan's general. Ormond barked his final commands and the knights dispersed in a clatter of metal on metal as they ran to do his bidding. Some went to gather riding gear and horses to try to head Zaltreous off before he could reach someone that might shelter him unknowingly in the outlying lands. Others went to double the numbers at their posts guarding the jewels, portcullis, ramparts and towers.

The din of the armour and shouting voices that called to each other eventually died down as the men settled into their new posts, and Oslan was finally able to talk to Ormond about what had happened. The prince bade Ormond meet with him in the war room to discuss strategy away from peasant ears that might overhear. Carn immediately fell into step beside Oslan, who objected. "Carn, you needn't coddle me like an infant. I do not need a guard twenty-four hours a day. While I talk with Ormond, the men will need someone they can turn to for further orders. Rest assured my general will keep me safe." He reasoned.

"Forgive me, but I wouldn't have the title of Royal Guard, Sire, if I failed to guard the royalty." Giving a slight bow of the head to Ormond, he continued, "I have all the faith in the world that you would be safe in Ormond's care, however, should the men find something, it should be him that decides what to do next. That is where his expertise lays." The prince sighed and accepted the fact that Carn would follow whether he liked it or not. Having Carn with him did make him feel slightly more secure. But it still made him feel like a child to have someone watching over him just in case a situation arose that he couldn't handle by himself.

Once at the armoury, and admitted by its guards, Oslan glanced at the place where Skirdkhen hung on the wall, to make sure it was still where it ought to be. Crossing the floor to the war room, he filled his general in about how Zaltreous had facilitated his escape by planting the draining packets on Carn, and warned him that now his men were up against a mage that had reclaimed his magic. Oslan rang for a servant, and sent him to convey to Aylan his need for her to attend the meeting, asking that she come at once if she was able. As the servant bustled out, the Queen, looking regal in her high necked gown, blew into the room and took a seat that Carn moved to hold for her. *How did she know?* Oslan thought incredulously. He had barely time to summon Aylan, and the Queen was already here.

"Don't look at me like a dragon with four heads, Oslan," she said emphatically, "I know about everything that goes on in my home. It is just one of the advantages of actually talking to servants, it is amazing the wealth of information that some of them hold."

Sometimes Oslan's mother infuriated him, but he stolidly kept his gaze levelled, not giving in to the desire to roll his eyes. It wouldn't do to allow for a foolhardy teenage whim, when he was trying to prove that he could handle the situation like the adult he was now expected to be.

"Did your servants happen to tell you how Zaltreous managed to get to his book?" Oslan inquired.

"I might be able to help with that." Aylan interjected as she entered the room, looking stronger than she had less than a half hour before. *Her strength must have returned quickly,* Oslan realized with relief.

"Go on," Queen Elsa encouraged, and Oslan realized with a little astonishment that this was the first time the Queen had been outwardly gracious to his fiancée.

"I went to examine Zaltreous' cell to see if I could figure it out on my own." Aylan continued, "I found the places in the wall that had contained my packets. Sure enough, they had all been removed. I also found a hole no bigger than the width of a thumb in the mortar covering the window. It was barely enough to see out of, but for Zaltreous, it would have been sufficient. He would have been able to cast on anyone in the square below that he could see. He could have made any one of them do his bidding under a spell from the *Almatraek Dim*."

"But he didn't have the book then," the queen pointed out, "How could he have cast from it without having it there to read from?"

Aylan looked down at the table putting her words in order before returning her gaze to the Queen. "Well, Your Majesty, if it was me," she said carefully, "and I found a spell that I liked quite a lot, I would try to memorize it." The room sat quiet for a few moments as those present tried to take that in. Aylan went on cautiously "It would be more difficult if it was a potion or paste that required a lot of strange or hard to find ingredients, but if it was simply an incantation, Zaltreous would be able to use it whenever he wished as long as he knew the words and had the power."

"But we have no way of knowing what spell he could have used." The queen concluded. Oslan caught his mage's gaze as she eyed him carefully, hesitating, but giving him a meaningful look. Silent communication passed between them, and he knew that she saw the change in his eyes as his face became grim with his reckoning.

"There is one we know of that he has used successfully in the past." She hedged.

"We know he used a possession spell before to control a man." Oslan spoke as a statement, without any question in his voice. He looked carefully at his mother. "It was the same one he used from the book to kill my father."

Chapter 14
~Escaping Reality~

In the days following the evil mage's escape, knights had been sent out as scouts to try to pick up his trail. So far, their searches had been unfruitful. Unbeknownst to them, Zaltreous had found his own kind of invisibility spell within the pages of the *Almatraek Dim*. It had caused him to blend in with the shadows, and in the dusk of the day of his escape when the shadows had grown long, he had walked right out of town past the guards and started his journey to the nearest village.

He had walked for days, mainly sticking to the forest that lined the road for cover. He had only his book and himself, and had soon become famished. The only food he was able to find had been some berries along the way, but they were hardly enough to sustain him. He knew nothing of hunting, and was rewarded with no meat when he attempted to kill a rabbit for his supper on the second day. He had little patience for waiting for the creatures, but when he had spotted one by chance he had opened the book to find a spell that would help him kill it. He had picked up a sharp twig and aimed it at the rabbit, and hoping against hope, he had incanted a spell that made the projectile fly at the bunny's head at a great speed. In the end, the alert rabbit had been quicker. Zaltreous was dumbfounded at its speed, it had been only a blur of fur through the forest and then it had been gone.

He had tried the same trick with a low flying bird, and had ended up eating a real meal for the first time since he had left Endalwynndale. His journey continued this way for over a week, when he was able to steal some apples from the first farmer's orchards on the outskirts of town.

Entering the town proper, his first thought had been only of food. He had been attempting to purchase a meal and some vital ingredients from a vendor in a store, waiting somewhat impatiently as there had been a long line ahead of him. When it had finally been his turn, a great fat pig of a man burst in through the door and began to order in a booming expectant voice as if the mage hadn't even been standing there. Zaltreous felt his hands clench into fists of rage. *What am I, still invisible?* He growled in his mind. Incensed as the man left with his order, Zaltreous forgot about the food and followed swiftly behind the insufferable man who had been referred to in the store as Lord Lapintal.

Not fifteen minutes later, Zaltreous considered the unconscious form sitting propped up in the corner of the lord's study. The man really had been a nuisance, with his pompous attitude and the way he put on airs in front of anyone who would listen. But things had worked out for the evil mage. Zaltreous had followed him all the way to his home, a great manor with a heavy wood door that had been no match for a simple spell. Zaltreous had snuck past the maids and servants and found the lord in an upstairs room full of books. *This place will do wonderfully,* he speculated. He confined Lapintal long enough to force him to order the servants out, and speculated what to do with him. However, as he drew closer to the squirming lord, the man fainted dead away out of fear. Now it appeared Zaltreous would have more time to decide what to do with him.

*   *   *

Oslan and Aylan had gone on a morning ride, deciding to spend some calming time as a couple amidst the stress of Zaltreous still being at large, and their upcoming union. Oslan had had a servant pack a picnic lunch, and they had been just setting out the repast when he had received a message to return from the queen. Now that all parties were satisfied with the match, she seemed to actually be looking forward to the big event. She might as well; she had just spent a small fortune and days of watching jesters, bards and other entertainers in order to prepare for the perfect occasion. He knew that this ceremony was important to her for he was her only son. He had therefore been content to let her take over, knowing that the wedding would be one fit for a king.

Oslan arrived home to find the whole palace decorated. Yards of bright fabrics were draped here and there to add an elegant touch, and he knew that his mother had been busy. The wedding was slated for the next day, and the servants were still bustling around as they made preparations and talked excitedly. From what he could gather, the local peasants had been put into a harvesting frenzy, trying to bring the queen only the freshest vegetables and even some apples for the grand meal that was to follow. Salt, honey, and many types of raised or hunted animals were brought in to supplement the feast. The queen looked kindly upon the couple, and welcomed them home before showering them with explanations of how the next day would proceed so the wedding would run smoothly.

Afterwards, with his head spinning once again with the onslaught of information, Oslan dragged himself upstairs. He was happy, yet worn and weary from the day's travelling and his mother's frantic barrage of what was to come. His personal servant Sherrod was waiting patiently in his chambers, ordering a hot bath to be brought and stoking the fire in the prince's outer room. The servant's nimble fingers deftly unfastened the prince's light armour, and Oslan's stomach twinged and growled loudly in the otherwise quiet room. "Majesty!" Sherrod exclaimed, "You haven't eaten?"

"We were only beginning to unpack lunch when we got an urgent message to come back." The prince replied, exhausted. Sherrod excused himself to bring the armour back to the armoury, and returned with a hot meal. A hearty stew, still piping hot, some bread, and tankard of ale were set on the writing desk for when the prince had finished bathing. Oslan thanked him, and a while later was tucked into bed clean, fed and content to think about the next day when he would finally make beautiful Aylan his wife. Though drowsy and comfortable under the warm blankets, it was a long time before Oslan could fall asleep, but when he finally did drift off, his dreams were sweet ones.

* * *

The evil mage's eye flicked quickly to the window to make sure the curtains were still closed. The heavy drapes afforded him little light, but he preferred the dark. He could always add light to a gloomy room if he needed to see better, but being enveloped in the dark made him feel secure. It was an advantage, especially when he was plotting; the dark meant no eyes prying into his affairs. He looked back down at the desk where he sat, a huge bowl of water acting as a scrying glass set before him. True, it worked about as well as any other reflective surface that could be used to see across leagues. With the right spell, one that he happened to be an expert at using, the water would show him anywhere or anyone in the world he asked to see. But it still wasn't the same. If the table was bumped, or if a fly flew into the liquid, it would distort the picture. He mourned the loss of his old mirror. Its theft was his first really dishonest act, and had perhaps set the tone for the rest of his life. The beautiful artifact had an oval glass, and its reflective surface was bordered by silver roses and leaves. Almost his most prized possession, only second to the book, it had been taken by the knights of Endalwynndale when he had been captured and jailed for his crimes. He intended to go back there to retrieve it, and pay the people of Endalwynndale back for their *hospitality*. He spat the word in his mind as he peered at the figures dancing on the surface of the water.

*　　　*　　　*

The next morning the prince awoke to a sun-filled day. His windows showed him blue skies with only the faintest wisps of clouds. The birdsong was loud and he could hear the market below in full bustle. Sherrod of course was there upon waking, preparing the prince's clothes across the room for the big day. Oslan stretched loudly, rustling the covers to unobtrusively let his servant know he was conscious again. The tall, slim man almost jumped, so deep in thought was he. Sherrod turned and bade the prince good morning with a stiff bow, and began laying down the law immediately.

"Now, Your Highness," he began, "I am told by the queen that you must remain in your chambers at least a little while longer. Your bride has gone to the market and you know what they say, a groom mustn't see the bride before the ceremony on the wedding day. We can't risk you catching a glimpse of her passing by in the halls. I shall return promptly with your breakfast."

Oslan sat somewhat stunned, never having seen Sherrod get excited about anything. True, the man wasn't as old as the prince's father had been, but his hair had begun to grey at the temples, and he always had a calm and collected manner about him. It was one of the reasons Oslan had kept him on for so long. Though he was stiff and proper, Sherrod was also always kind. The prince sighed heavily and resigned himself to pacing across his quarters until Sherrod returned.

Chapter 15
~ All in the Delivery ~

In Lapintal's manor, the sharp noise of the door's metal knocker striking its iron plate sounded through the vast foyer. Zaltreous heard the impatient *tak-tak-tak* below and looked contemptuously at the lord, now conscious, gagged and bound to a chair in the corner of the room. The little man was fat and balding, with hair that grew only around the sides and back of his head. His face was like a squished turnip; round, with a bulbous nose, chubby cheeks, and a double chin dissected by a deep crevasse. Zaltreous, a man that had always secretly been vain about his looks, hated the idea of appearing as this man for even a moment. As the knocking from below became more insistent, he quickly flipped through the *Almatraek Dim*. He scanned the pages and was rewarded as he found the perfect spell for this situation. He read it over, found the powerful centre of energy at his core, and focusing on the burning, swirling orb, willed branches of it outward, and incanted in Almatrae. Within the blast of energy he created, his body transformed around him. His clothes tore as he began to fill out in the middle, gaining pounds in mere minutes what it had taken Lapintol years to accumulate. Tears sprang from the mage's blue eyes as the spell made his skin stretch before it began shortening his bones painfully. Finally, panting, and clenching his teeth against the intense pain, the spell finished by changing his hair and face. The whole process took only moments, but it felt to Zaltreous like it had been an eternity.

He almost winded himself by trying to cross the room to dress too quickly, and realized that this spell was more dangerous than anticipated.

Normally lean and fit, his newfound girth had slowed him substantially, and his heart was beating fit to burst from the simple exertion. *How can someone live like this?* He silently cursed, and made a note to take the stairs slowly, so he would not die of a heart attack on the way down.

Normally, a servant would have answered the door in a manor such as this, but Zaltreous had forced Lapintal to give them all time off. They might have gone away thinking that was strange enough, but the more Zaltreous used magic, the more he risked being found out. Mages were rare in this kingdom, and most subjects either feared it or didn't really believe magic existed at all. If they were to encounter it first hand, most folk would have rumours spread around the town before he realized a servant was onto him. Besides, it was much easier to keep a man bound in a room when there was no one around to hear him call for help.

Zaltreous made it to the ground floor with some difficulty, and was huffing and puffing by the time he had waddled over to open the door. He daubed at his sweaty forehead with a handkerchief as it swung open. He gasped for breath, and waited while an old man in a white robe far too big for him handed over an envelope. His almost black eyes sparkled with some deep seated knowledge, and seemed almost too young for all the folds of wrinkles on his face. A plain rope was tied at his waist as a belt, and the whole man seemed almost shrunken in stature. Even though Zaltreous in Lapintal's form was much shorter than usual, this man was even still a head shorter than that.

"My mistress wishes to see you, whoever you are!" The old man said with glee.

"I am Lord Lapintal." Zaltreous replied while taking the envelope.

The man seemed to try to straighten despite his hunched back, his long white scraggly hair waving back and forth furiously as he did. He managed to gain one or two more inches of height as he rose onto his toes, allowing him to stand almost eye to gleaming eye with Zaltreous before he intoned in a low voice, "Next time read your spell more carefully boy, Lapintal has brown eyes."

Before Zaltreous could react, the little man had resumed his stooped posture and had begun to hobble away down the avenue. *I swear that man is cackling!* Zaltreous thought, stunned to the bone at the man's revelation.

He closed the heavy wooden door and tried once again to travel far too quickly across the room for his heavy form. Grasping the heavy stair post long enough to catch his breath, he set off again, breaking out in a hot sweat as he half raced in a quick waddle up the stairs which he could no longer take two at a time. Flinging open the door to the office where the real Lapintal was being held captive, Zaltreous moved to where the fat man was tied to the chair by invisible bonds of magic. With a grunt, he lowered himself so he could peer into the man's eyes, both faces for a split second like a mirror image of confusion and suspicion. "Taus," *Sleep,* Zaltreous intoned as he waved his palm over the pudgy man's bulging eyes. The man's head drooped slightly as the folds of his chin made contact with his meaty chest in a deep slumber.

The mage moved to the huge leather-bound book laying opened on the table. He read through the spell again, only now taking time to check the small cursive writing at the bottom of the page. *Beware, the eyes are the windows of the soul,* it said in Almatrae, *and cannot be changed so easily,*

For closer encounters, leave nothing to chance. Use another spell to shroud or change the eyes. "How cryptic," he complained, "I will find a way to remedy this spell's unfortunate downfall."

Zaltreous went to the master bedroom where he found a large mirror hanging on the wall. His own piercing ice blue eyes stared back at him above fat cheeks, which were now rosy with exertion. *Apparently, someone else has tried the same trick before,* he thought mirthlessly, *I wonder, what was their fate?* Zaltreous counted himself lucky that this meeting was only with a messenger, and no one of consequence. The ramblings of an old man were easy to ignore even if he did decide to tell someone. Zaltreous had been very lucky indeed, although, he had recognized the magic. Fearful, Zaltreous pondered, *How had he known, and who's ears might listen?*

Chapter 16
~ Vows ~

The hour had come when Oslan's family and Aylan's were to be joined together. Oslan waited impatiently at the base of the garden's scaled dragon tongue tree as Thorn and his minstrels played his parents' wedding song. The prince hadn't seen Aylan all day long, and as the hour grew closer, he had grown anxious for it to happen all the sooner. Cool and collected as he forced himself to appear on the outside, the waiting was killing him. He was to be a king in under a week, yet that was child's play. This was to be his wedding night and he felt totally unprepared for what lay ahead.

He let his gaze follow the ruby red carpet runner up the length of the garden path, reminding himself not to squint in order to catch the first glimpse of Aylan before anyone else. He could feel the weight of hundreds of pairs of eyes that were scrutinizing him as he waited, full of anticipation and stone still, with his fingertips lightly plastered to his legs to prevent himself from fidgeting. Other guests stared approvingly at the blooming tree behind him and it's plethora of decorations. The trunk was a deep green, bumpy with scales akin to those of a dragon. The branches split and split again into twos, forming hundreds of gaping mouths from which spewed bright yellow and red leaves and orange flowers like eyes where the small fruit would soon form. Vines draped from branch to branch, and hung down like thin tails. With the sun shining through the mighty tree, it gave off the look of being on fire. As was the tradition in this kingdom, the children in the town had made decorations to hang on the tree to wish the bride and groom wealth and fertility, and parents lifted them to the lower branches to hang what they had made. Husbands and wives looked upon the bright leaves and their wedding tattoos in memory of their own joinings.

Oslan was dressed in impressive clothes designed for today by his sisters. As was tradition, the bride and groom's outfits were made to match the colour of their eyes, and since it was too hard to match the rare green-brown amber colour of Oslan's irises, the tailors had outdone themselves by creating a material that appeared to be green when looked at from one angle, and brown from the other. As he moved, the clothing looked as fluid as his gaze. Black obsidian stones like pupils were sewn into the high collar, and continued down from the shoulders in a v-line to the waist. The eyes were said to be the window to the soul, and on this day, the couple would symbolically bare their souls to each other, showing a flawless purity of their love for one another. Wedding garments had to be sewn perfectly, and the material must remain completely unblemished. Tailors made a reputation for themselves by completing the intricate patterns of stitching that would make each garment memorable and unique.

An appreciative gasp rose up from the crowd announcing Aylan's entrance at the far end of the garden's path. She walked at Lorelyn's side, the proud mother letting her tears of joy flow unhindered down her rosy cheeks. Aylan wore what seemed to be a simple dress of blue that shimmered like flowing water as she walked, unexpected and wonderful. Her blonde hair was piled in a banded tower of curls atop her head, which she held up at a regal angle as she approached the tree. The dragon's breath in her bouquet added to a mixture of colours that seemed to spill from her hands without being dropped. She smiled and pink bloomed in her cheeks as her eyes found his. His heart soared, *perfection itself,* was the only phrase that came to his mind to describe her. As she came close enough to take his hand, he saw that her dress was not as plain as he had originally thought. Crystal blue and white gems cascaded across the bodice, and had been sewn into the hem and trim of her dress causing the rippling effect. The pattern of the jewels glittered in a repeating pattern that matched the leaves of the dragon tongue tree. Her hand found his and all of his fears melted away.

Marriage ceremonies were usually presided over by the lord of a given town, making the union legal. In the case of the royal wedding, the king or queen would conduct the ceremony for their children. Oslan's mother motioned for them to raise their joined hands to hers. She separated their hands and reached up to pull a sprig from the tree above her head. She took the red and yellow leaf and delicately placed it on Oslan's upturned palm. She had Aylan put her hand on top of Oslan's, sandwiching the leaf between them. Then a servant brought a vine from the tree, which Elsa wove between their fingers and spiraled around their joined hands to the wrist, binding them together.

"Now you must sing the words." The queen instructed. Oslan felt his palm begin to sweat beneath the leaf. This was the moment he had been dreading. The people of his kingdom always expected great things of their prince, and to date, he had always been able to pleasantly surprise them. He had avoided practicing his vows with Aylan out of embarrassment even though it was to be done in Almatrae, and she was fluent in the language. Now that the moment had arrived, he was afraid that he was about to lose some of the esteem she and his subjects held him in.

Oslan had loved music, but had been put off singing as a young child when he had been playing by the kennels one day. He had been belting out a jaunty tune, copying a court bard he had once heard sing a magnificent song. The dogs reacted. They all started to howl, and his favourite dog, Pacer, had started whining while he sung. The kennel master had appeared and told him to "Cut the racket, lest I set the dogs loose to cut it themselves. Can't you see they're in pain boy?" He had treated Oslan as if he had hurt them, he had believed it, and it had broken his kind heart, so he had never sung again...until today.

Queen Elsa took the couple and walked them closer to the tree. She motioned for them to raise their bonded hands, so their fingertips pointed up toward the tree's foliage, and the edge of their hands rested against its trunk. Oslan felt the bumpy, scaled bark beneath his skin and steeled himself for what was to come next. The minstrels began to play the song that would bind them to the tree and each other, and mercifully, Aylan began, weaving the marriage spell.

> *"Ey plate ot Tay eyt furiela est ilao,*
> *Est tut jus nae gollay,*
> *Eyt jutaile taroxae joliya taroxae tao,*
> *Ey gor eyt ilaola ot Tay."*

> *I pledge to thee my life and heart,*
> *And honesty until we part,*
> *My faithfulness will always be true,*
> *I give my love to you.*

Her voice was carrying and beautiful, and Oslan was filled with a burst of pride that helped to quell the fear building up inside him. Perhaps this would be alright after all. The musicians continued to play the song that had already begun to awaken the energy in the tree. The broken vine snaked down toward the couple, rejoining itself to the piece around their hands. It started to glow and changed to an intense bright red, lighting the leaf between their palms.

The crown prince's lips parted, and he began making his promise that would join him to his wife. What came out was simply astonishing. To their credit, the troubadours continued to play, though with rictus expressions on their faces as if trying to ignore a bad smell. The prince was hopelessly tone deaf. A small child in the front row immediately covered his ears with both hands, and his mother rushed to lower his arms and coo to the child so he wouldn't make a fuss in front of the crowd. Oslan only stumbled a bit near the beginning when on the first note, he could feel Aylan's hand tighten in momentary shock, but her eyes found his and comforted him, and she nodded her encouragement for him to continue. By the brightness, he loved this woman.

Miraculously, the out of tune singing did not affect the spell on the tree. The vine seemed to melt into their skin. There was the flash of a cutting sensation, and then it was gone, leaving only a slight tingling behind. Oslan felt the hair on the back of his neck begin to rise, and a slight sense of vertigo overtook him as the spell took hold. As the last notes of the song played, the glow disappeared, and

Oslan regarded his newly marked hand. He saw Aylan too, admiring the way the vine curled around them, as if it were still wrapped around their joined hands. The bright leaf had disappeared from between their palms, and he felt her warm dry hand against his. On the wrist, the leaf now showed as a symbol of their union. No two marriage patterns were alike, and only Aylan's vine tattoo would match up with Oslan's, proving they were a couple. If one of them died, the leaf would fade from sight, but the markings of the vine would always remain.

The Queen announced to the crowd that the couple was wed, and a cheer went up as they turned to the tree to select one of the ornaments that hung there. This was an old tradition in Endalwynndale, dating back to the second king. The newly wedded couple would select a decoration, and upon having a baby, they would name their child after the one that had made the ornament. This meant that there were some very old names that still lived on in the people of the kingdom, but it also allowed for new names to be created if the family bore a child of a different gender. This had been the case for Oslan's youngest sister. The name Trindalynn had been made anew when her parents had pulled an ornament from the tree that bore the name of a boy named Trindol.

Oslan looked up into the bright leaves of red and yellow, searching for a decoration that would stand out. There were so many, how was he to choose? He saw paper decorations in the shapes of hand prints, little dolls made out of straw and horse hair, and bits of ribbon with buttons sewn on them. Older children had done impressive embroidery, or fashioned things out of metal that clinked on the breeze as the pieces touched. Then he saw it, a simple attempt at embroidery obviously done by a young child. He reached up to grasp it and hesitated, realizing that this was a decision, like the rest to follow, that he must make with his wife. He looked to her, but her hand was already reaching for the very ornament he had chosen. They brought it down together, looking at the artwork as a sigh was released from the crowd. It was a small square of cloth no bigger than the prince's palm. The edges were rough, and the stitching uneven. A falcon stared back at them, eyes almost bulging, too large wings raised above a fat tummy, with tiny yellow feet hanging down. Underneath were two words formed as one in awkward off kilter stitching: swiftwing. Oslan called out to the crowd, holding it up for all to see. "Which child will be the namesake for the future ruler of this kingdom?"

"I will," came a small but brave voice from among the guests. A girl with blond curly hair and dirt on her face walked on bare feet, up the centre isle that Aylan had used a short time before. A small swatch of material was missing from the bottom of her dress. It matched their decoration. Oslan's heart went out to her, and Aylan reached down to pick the child up, ignoring the fact that the child's dirt might rub off on her wedding gown. The girl automatically raised her arms to be lifted, and settled into the circle of Aylan's arms quite comfortably.

"Is this your name?" Oslan asked the girl, pointing at the word.

"No, silly, that's the *bird's* name." She said confidently. The guests that could hear her laughed softly.

"Well I think that's a fine name for a bird." Aylan replied. The girl smiled and nodded, obviously pleased. "But, what is your name?"

"She looked at the prince, then at his wife,

and then looked down, feeling awkward.

"Oh, it can't be that bad," Oslan encouraged. She looked up earnestly into Oslan's eyes and he could see colour rushing into her face. The poor little thing was embarrassed.

"I have a boy's name." She confided.

"Well let's hear it," Aylan prompted, "I'm sure we will love it as much as your parents must love you." The child sighed a heavy sigh and motioned to be put down. She took a step back and told them her name.

"Thrush," the girl said quietly. The onlookers grew silent, waiting to see what the reaction would be.

"Well, Thrush," Oslan responded, "We will use the name with pride." The crowd roared its approval with applause and shouts.

Thrush beamed at that, bowed to the audience, curtseyed to the couple, and scampered back into the crowd.

Chapter 17
~ Gifts ~

"Now for the gifts!" the queen announced exuberantly with a brisk clap of her hands. The minstrels stepped off of their stage and allowed the couple and queen to take their place. It was customary for a newly wedded bride and groom to present each other with a token of their responsibility within the relationship. It said that both people were looking to make contributions and would help support each other, and a new gift was the sign of a new start. It was also tradition that until the giving, that it be kept as a secret, to show that for each surprise life gave them, they would face it together.

Oslan glanced at his mage and swelled with pride, he knew Aylan would love his gift. He had spent a fair amount of coin on it, and it was something that he knew she had wanted, though she would never approach him on the subject of her getting one due to the cost. He had had it imported from the desert lands of Embral, and when it had arrived, he could see that it had been worth every penny. He nodded a signal, and a servant entered wearing a sturdy brown leather glove. Upon the glove sat a pristine saker falcon. The various shades of brown feathers marked with grey-white would have helped it blend in with the desert sands, and would help it here blend in with the dappled light in the forest and fields where Oslan loved to hunt. Aylan clapped her hands and bounced up and down in a decidedly childlike reaction to the gift. That was alright, Oslan speculated that it hadn't been all that long ago when they had been considered children. The saker glared at the jumping human uneasily and let out a shrill "Kiy-ee!"

The guests let out an appreciative "Oh!" and began to babble about the impressive gift. Oslan smiled and held out an object wrapped in cloth, which Aylan excitedly unwrapped. Inside, was an expertly tailored black glove to match the one Oslan used with his falcon, Archer. She placed it on her hand, and approached the falcon slowly. She took the bird's jesses from the servant, and felt the bird transfer its weight to her arm as it stepped onto her glove. It stood a full nineteen inches high, so that standing on her arm it could almost look her in the eye. She noticed that the brown feathering on its face made it look almost as though it were wearing a mask. "Oh Oslan, he's beautiful." She crooned.

"What will you name him?" Oslan asked. Without hesitation, she answered him, "Swiftwing, the same name as the bird on Thrush's swatch of cloth."

Oslan watched and waited in anticipation as she returned Swiftwing to the servant, who would take it to the mews in the tower where the other falcons lived. It was now his turn to receive the gift she had prepared for him. He had no idea what the gift might be, but he speculated that it could be a powder or potion that she had concocted with magical properties. In previous years, she and her handmaid had gotten up to some antics with an invisibility pill she had created under Lazelan's direction. He secretly hoped it would be something as useful.

He watched his new wife nod to Thorn, who turned to talk briefly with one of the minstrels. *What is this?* Wondered Oslan, *she can't have tried to write a song of her own!* But instead of a flowery love song, out came a blasting of horns that signaled the entrance of a few of Oslan's knights. Ormond, the commander in chief of Oslan's army, led the procession himself, tall and powerfully built.

His knights were carrying the giant tower shields that had been the cause of the expression many in the kingdom used. He was followed by Carn, Bowregard, Trembleton, and three other knights that Oslan had only recently raised to the flame. The squires that followed carried a sparring dummy over their heads. *How very unusual, what is this?* Oslan wondered once again. His curiosity peaked as the squires set up the training dummy before the crowd, and Ormond approached him. From behind his great shield he pulled a colourful smaller version, but warned Oslan not to touch it.

The saliva seemed to leave Oslan's mouth as it went dry, and he was rendered speechless. He swallowed hard, knowing full well that the crowd was watching for his reaction. The thing had a blasted flower of all things painted in the dead centre of the red and blue background. It looked like it had been finely crafted by a master armour-smith, but still, did she really expect him to carry around such a feminine implement of war? He supposed he could always bring it to tea with the queen.

"And now a brief demonstration." His crazy wife announced. Outwardly, he plastered what he hoped resembled an interested, joyful smile on his face, while inwardly, he groaned. He could see the puzzled faces of the onlookers, and saw one of the squires elbow another and point at the shield, barely able to contain a snicker. *These two will have to learn some propriety,* Oslan thought, perhaps he had made a mistake to give them a chance at their flames.

Ormond stood ready for the presentation, facing the practice dummy, unarmed except for the prince's new flowery atrocity. Twenty feet away, from behind the practice dummy, Bowregard readied his bow and drew an arrow from the quiver he wore at his back. This had been a specially made arrow for this occasion, with a packet over the tip to blunt it from damaging the new shield. Aylan surveyed the scene from Oslan's side, then motioned for Bowregard to move back an additional ten feet. Oslan shifted his weight impatiently. He already had a perfectly good shield of his own that he loved, he hoped she'd excuse him from using this new monstrosity. Perhaps he could get away with hanging it decoratively in the throne room, that way he could argue more people could admire it. Yes, that might just work.

"In the centre of the shield is a dragon's breath flower, like the ones I wear in my hair. I thought it would be appropriate to match the dragon sword that you carry." She explained. Oh great, now that she had brought Skirdkhen into this, he would have to use the shield in public while he wielded the sword. Hopefully he could avoid using it at a tournament with his people watching, perhaps he could use it in battle; the enemy might laugh themselves to death before he even need fight them. The thought amused and comforted him. Then Bowregard let loose his arrow, which flew past the dummy toward Ormond. It hit the bottom metal tip of the shield with a hollow *ping*.

"Watch it there laddy!" Ormond thundered, "I'll not lose my knees to ya!" Colouring, Bowregard apologised to Aylan, "Forgive me Highness, I am not yet used to the extra weight of the packets that tip my bow." She turned to speak softly to her prince.

"I'm sorry, Love, one more try," Aylan promised, "We'll get it this time."

"No, really, that's ok, I can see the um...beauty and craftsmanship of this...stunning gift." Oslan stammered quietly to her, willing her to end this whole charade now. He was hungry and he wanted to get to the feast. He would just ask her to make him an invisibility pill at a later time, when her feelings wouldn't be hurt.

"You haven't seen anything yet." Aylan replied as Bow loosed his second arrow. There was a quick flash of the arrow, this time travelling just over the shoulder of the practice dummy, and a solid *thunk* as it landed square in the centre of the dragon's breath. Fire immediately erupted from the shield's surface, spewing forth a twenty foot cascade of flame that incinerated the practice dummy instantly. Oslan forgot his opposition to the flower as his jaw hung agape. It was blooming magnificent, he would carry it always! "Does it do that every time?" He asked hopefully.

"Yes, my Love. That is why the flower is so big, so you have the best chance of using my enchantment. You didn't think I'd just give you a plain old shield without any magic, did you?" She asked wryly.

Chapter 18
~ The Mystery of a Note ~

Zaltreous peered angrily at the pages before him. He had once again taken the guise of Lord Lapintal, though he had still not figured out a way around the problem of concealing the colour of the eyes. The *Almatraek Dim* seemed to hold no solutions, and Zaltreous hadn't been taught anything in his classes that would suffice. That was the problem with studying at a university as he had; they tended to teach you spells that would only be useful for do-gooders. He withdrew the stiff envelope from under the cover of the heavy tome, noting that the cream coloured paper was fine indeed. His now pudgy fingers slid the heavy paper out from its snug paper pocket, with some difficulty. Unfolding it, he read the flowing script in wonder for what seemed like the hundredth time.

Mysterious Stranger,

Join me at my estate on the morrow at noon. I will send my servant, Flanx, with a carriage to spare you the journey by foot. You have something I desire. If you would be so kind as to bring Lapintal with you, I would be much obliged.

A.

Grimacing, he refolded it and began incanting the same spell he had used on himself, this time directed at Lapintal, tied as he was in his chair. Extending his palm and splayed fingers toward the obese wriggling lord, Zaltreous sent energy from his core toward his mark. Lapintal went stiff as the hair on the back of his neck started to rise, then redoubled his efforts to squirm out of his bonds as the magic began to take its effect. As his body began to shrivel, he howled while his considerable bulk began to turn in on itself. When the spell was complete, Lapintal resembled one of the older guards that used to stand outside Zaltreous' cell.

In order to shift someone's shape into another's, the caster had to both see the person he was to transform, and also be able to envision the new shape quite clearly in his mind. Otherwise, the spell would still work, changing the person under its influence, but the new form would seem wrong somehow, a little fuzzy around the edges, and the shape wouldn't hold very well. Zaltreous had seen much of the old guard stationed outside his cell, had in fact stared at him for hours trying to psych him out by feigning casting ability when the packets had in fact made him unable to cast for so long. The sentry had been sharp, and his wrinkled face had stopped showing concern after the first few attempts, but what else was a powerless mage supposed to have done with his time locked away if not to play with the minds of those guarding him.

Zaltreous finished with the spell, leaving Lapintal in a sagging, panting heap, and reached for the *Almatraek Dim*. The tome closed with a puff of dust and a sound like thunder. He hurriedly did up the buckles on the cover that held the book closed while he looked around for his bag. Upon seeing its scuffed and aged appearance, however, he realized that it would never do for a lord. He asked Lapintal where his own bag might be, but the now aged man replied disdainfully that he would never carry a bag, that was what servants were for.

Zaltreous hesitated, then slid the large

volume into his own satchel, and folded the top over to cover it. He used magic to unbind his prisoner, and looped the strap of the bag over the lord's head. "Then you shall be my servant," Zaltreous informed him sternly. Lapintal began to splutter, but Zaltreous grabbed the weak flailing man by the scruff of the neck, and began his slow trek down the stairs taking care not to work up a sweat. All he needed was for his slick hand to slip on the handrail, causing his great form to topple down the stairs to land in a quivering injured mass. He seriously doubted that with this girth, he would be able to rise from a prone position to get help if that were the case.

He dragged Lapintal unceremoniously along behind him, uncaring if the man bumped walls or stairs, and gave no thought whatever to the many slivers his captive may be amassing as he stumbled repeatedly to the wooden floors.

Zaltreous' thoughts returned to the mysterious letter he had folded into his large pocket. Whoever the note was from, he reasoned, if they could spare a carriage and servant to come get him, they must be nobility. It made him all the more eager to meet with them. He was getting used to having a lord's manor at his disposal, and who knew what wealth this mysterious person who had simply signed the note as *A* might hold.

The script suggested a woman's hand, although someone with enough money might have a servant to do his correspondence for him. Still, with a message such as this, he guessed whomever this *A* person was, they had probably written it themselves. Either that or he had trusted minions to do his bidding, something else Zaltreous was curious about.

He had often thought he could use some

trustworthy help, but how to find it was the question. When there were so many who might squeal on him at even the slightest provocation, how was he to know who could be trusted or who would run to the authorities, causing him to suffer an inconvenient blow for his troubles. No, whoever had written this note to him must be powerful indeed, after all, the note's author had known about him taking over the manor, and it hadn't escaped the mage's notice that in the letter, A, had referred to Lapintal as just that. There had been no lord honorific attached to his name.

Zaltreous huffed and puffed down the last few steps, and heaved the bedraggled Lapintal over the stone floor to the door just as someone used the heavy knocker on the other side of it. The sound was an insistent and almost deafening *tak-tak-tak*! He pulled the lord to his feet and allowed him a brief moment to brush some of the dust and splinters free from his clothing.

"We are going to walk to the awaiting carriage out front." Zaltreous hissed into Lapintal's ear. "If you should get any ideas about bolting on me, I swear to you that you will mourn the loss of the use of your legs when my magic catches up to you!" Lapintal eyed Zaltreous uneasily, but in his aged form, Zaltreous doubted the lord could hobble much faster than he could in his newfound girth. Besides, he wouldn't have to run after the smaller man, his magic had a far reach.

Zaltreous' chubby face burst into a dazzling smile a mere second before he pulled the heavy bolt on the door free from its bracket. The door swung inward, revealing a miserably rainy day. Zaltreous found himself face to face with the waterlogged version of the same strange stooped man that had visited him on the previous day.

"Ah, I see you are ready! It is well then, let's be off," the smaller man suggested happily, motioning with one arm toward a sleek black wooden, covered carriage. A team of four perfectly white horses harnessed to the carriage seemed to almost shimmer with the wet droplets refracting from their backs. One tossed its head impatiently, and another pawed at the ground with its heavy hoof, though the carriage did not roll an inch. It gave Zaltreous an uncanny feeling to see them. Something wasn't quite right about the image, but he couldn't put his finger on what.

To Zaltreous' relief, Lapintal walked meekly to the carriage, even if he was taking furtive glances at freedom the whole way. Zaltreous supposed that had anyone been around, Lapintal might have caused some trouble, but as it happened, it was a rather quiet morning with no one afoot. The servant, Flanx, according to the note, held the door for them and then shut them securely inside before scrambling up to the bench where he would drive the team home. The carriage creaked slightly as it bumped along the well-worn unpaved roads. Its occupants were jostled, but the rich cushions on their seat kept the journey from being too uncomfortable. Every now and then Zaltreous allowed Lapintal to pull back the heavy curtains on the door's window panel so they could see their progress through Entwhilen's countryside.

After an hour, the carriage passed a well-built stone wall, and the rough plains became well-tended fields and meadows. The horses' hooves clip-clopped over a stone bridge as they made their way over a sizeable creek, and they seemed to speed a little, sensing that their warm, dry stable was near. Trees began to line the drive, and they passed yet another stone wall made directly around what could only be described as a small fortress.

As the carriage drew nearer, a thought popped into Zaltreous' mind like the flashing of a candle sparking to life. The horses...they had been pawing at the ground in the pouring rain outside Lapintal's manor, yet there hadn't been a drop of mud on their perfectly white legs. *Another mage then*, Zaltreous reasoned, and decided to guard his book all the more carefully.

Chapter 19
~ Singing out ~

Later that evening when the eating and drinking were through, Oslan held his wife's hand as he led her toward the garden for the reception's dance. After a heavy feast that he had only eaten half of out of nervousness for what was to come later, it felt wonderful to be able to exchange a quiet word with her now. "I thought today would never come," he confessed. "Now you are a princess and my wife, and will soon be my queen. I feel that I am standing in a whirlwind of joy."

They had arrived in the centre of the dance floor, amid the heady odour of flowers and the rustle of rich fabrics of the guests around them. The sound of crickets filled the cool night air and Oslan became aware of goose bumps prickling up on Aylan's arms. He smoothed his palms along her cool skin, warming it, and felt them begin to recede. Goblets of honey mead were circulated to the guests and cups were raised for a toast. Thorn addressed the newly wedded couple:

"Prince Oslan, the *Endalwynndale Enchantment* was composed for King Eurilas and Queen Elsa's wedding day. Tonight I would like to present you with your own song to take you not only into your rein as our next worthy ruler, but also into your new long and all-willing bright and happy life together." A cheer went up among the revelers, and the goblets were drained. Oslan bowed in response, acknowledging the fine gift Thorn had managed to have kept a secret. The sweet chords of music seemed to float on the breeze as the minstrels began to pluck out a tune of brilliance and lulling comfort. Oslan found it easy to sway with Aylan in and out of complex dance patterns that would mark the moves to this song for the rest of the kingdom. Thorn sang:

"When the couple first did meet, the prince stood up above,
And watched a girl in the marketplace that was to be his love.
Her temperament, so virtuous, she foiled a thief with fire,
And up above within his chambers he could see her ire.

He had her brought before him then, to meet this freckled child,
Who burst into his chambers with an attitude all but mild,
He offered her some steaming tea, which she sprayed in his face,
When he told her she'd be by his side in his father's mage's place.

She learned the art of magic and her feelings then did swerve,
She thought she saw the prince's eye upon her every curve.
Tis true she grew into the lass you see before you now,
But even then the prince was smitten with her anyhow.

The clash and clangs rang in the air as Oslan learned his craft,
So dashing in his armour and very rarely ever daft,
He asked her for her token when he was upon the field,
Romancing her, he kissed his love, and then the deal was sealed.

A fairer pair has never been to be the country's rule,
And as a mage, our princess now, will be a radiant tool,
And happy days are yet to come from Oslan's swift command,
And Aylan's as our newfound Queen, who sits at his right hand."

As they danced, the prince's cheeks grew hot upon remembering the interview he had shared with her the first day they had met. Her cheeks coloured too at the embarrassing memory, so Oslan drew Aylan's attention away to the tiny flitting sparks of fireflies rising up in the garden all around them. It was as if the two of them were dancing among the stars. His heart swelled with a happiness he had not felt in a long time, and he thought he could imagine his pulse beating in time with hers. As the notes lingered in the air around the couple at the song's close, he reluctantly let her go for the few moments it would take to applaud Thorn's efforts.

The rejoicing continued on into the night, and Oslan knew that the next day was going to be a long one given the planning for his upcoming coronation, not to mention the fact that he expected that tonight he would receive very little sleep indeed.

As the number of dancing couples began to dwindle, Oslan grew more nervous about what was to come in their bed chamber. This was his wedding night after all, and the few kisses he'd shared with Aylan had been the only physical experience he'd ever had with a girl. He didn't want to disappoint her.

When the guests had left, they walked together with her arm laced through his, up the staircase that led to their awaiting room. He was glad that she wasn't holding his hand. His palms were beginning to sweat, and he was fairly sure that if she touched them she would be able to detect the slight shaking in them. *At least I'm in shape,* he proudly thought while remembering some of the men that had come to woo his sister. *I have all my hair and teeth, and I bathed earlier today, all in all, I'm quite a catch!* He reassured himself.

They entered the bed chambers to find candles lighting it, and a rather large tub of lazily steaming hot water waiting. *Only one tub! May brightness guide my way,* he silently prayed. The room smelled of lilacs, the scent his wife always added to her baths wafting up on the steam. Sherrod had done his homework. Oslan closed and barred the door behind them and noticed her nervously stealing a glance at him. *Maybe she is as unsure as I am,* he contemplated, *this might be alright after all.* Reminding himself that this was her first time too, he was able to relax a little.

He subconsciously wiped his palms off on his clothes before reaching forward for hers. When her fingers touched his ever so timidly, he felt his skin tingle wherever they made contact on his palm. He was aware that his breathing was slow and shaky as he pulled her closer to him.

"You once told me that you thought my kisses were all for the sake of a game, and that you wished that I would kiss you in earnest." Colour flooded her cheeks but she nodded shyly and he continued. "I hope today has proven to you that I mean this as no game," he loosed one of her hands and laced his fingers behind her neck through her intricate hair. He let go of her other hand and found her waist. She rested her palms on his shoulders as he pulled her yet closer so their foreheads rested together. "I love you, Aylan, with every fibre of my being, and I swear to you that whether I ever again kiss you for a game or for true, I will mean every one that follows this."

He watched her eyes slide shut as they drew together, and he joined her in blissful darkness that heightened the sensation of her soft lips against his. They moved together, ignoring the tub, taking steps toward the huge four post bed. He let his fingers release her hair and trail their tips down the side of her neck so that they barely made contact. She whimpered a lost happy sound deep in her throat and a sense of joyful wonder surprised him as her hands curled into his short locks and she kissed him hungrily.

He was intoxicated by the smell of lilacs on her skin as he reached around to unfasten her dress. Then panic hit as he realized that he had no idea how to undo a lady's gown. From the feel of it, it was all cords and eyelets. His fingers felt lost in a maze of zig-zagging laces. He pulled back, and wondered if he looked as flushed and dishevelled as she did. He grinned at her as she tried to pull him back into the embrace.

"I appreciate your enthusiasm, in fact, I would really like to remove these garments so we can get closer, but you're very distracting, and I must be able to see what I'm doing."

Relenting, she turned her back to him and he felt his jaw drop as he saw what his fingers had felt. *What am I supposed to do with this?* He panicked. Things were going so well, he didn't want to lose the mood. But...this? Her gown was laced from the back of her neck to the small of her back. Beautifully shimmering fabric was brought together with white cords like small ropes made for this sort of thing. Oslan had often admired their criss-crossing patterns, but never had to deal with undoing the blasted things. This could potentially take hours...if he could even get the knot at the bottom undone. He began to fumble with the cords where they were fastened together and quickly gave up.

"Do you want me to call Millie to undo the dress?" Aylan asked helpfully.

Hmm, let me think about that, was his mind's immediate response, *do I want to invite my wife's maid in here to help me get my wife out of her clothes on our wedding night? I would be the laughing stock of the kingdom in hours!* What he said was: "That's all right dear, I can manage." With that, he gave up trying to undo the knot and bent at the waist, almost taking a knee. With one fluid motion, he rose, pulling a dagger from where it resided in his boot, and sliced upward, severing all the laces in one go. Her dress almost fell off of her.

He took a moment to admire the curve of her spine and the creamy skin of her perfect back before tossing the dagger onto the desk by the wall. He spun her around to face him once more, and she stumbled over the pool of material caught around her legs. Now her gown fell off in earnest, and she did the first thing she could think of to cover up in embarrassment; she pressed herself against him in a desperate hug.

Works for me! He thought thankfully after being unsure as to how to get her back into his arms. Her touch was electric fire that awakened in him a need that he hadn't felt before. He wrapped his arms around her in earnest, sheltering her, and lifting her out of her gown and up onto the bed. He was very aware of her warmth pressed against him, and the rest of the night flowed in a smooth progression of passion and love.

Later, as he drifted off into sleep with his

new bride in his arms, he lay thinking. He had believed that his favourite sound in the world had been when Aylan spoke Almatrae, the exotic language of magic. As it turned out, he had been wrong. There was one that was even better: the sound of her voice singing out his name.

Chapter 20
~ Meeting One's Match ~

The carriage finally came to a halt in front of an entryway that looked as equally impressive as Lapintal's had been. A snarling lion's head held a ring between its jaws as the door's knocker. Zaltreous found that he was holding his breath in anticipation as Flanx climbed down from the carriage's driving bench, and proceeded to open the carriage door for the disguised mage and noble. The bent man hobbled ahead of them, and ignoring the impressive knocker, opened the door and entered. Once his two guests were safely inside, Flanx shut the door behind them and led them back through the small castle.

Zaltreous' mind was flying through figures as he took in the rich tapestries, ornate furniture and even servants milling about. *Servants!* He thought incredulously, *perhaps I have misjudged this meeting, although the tone of the letter had certainly seemed secretive. Perhaps Lapintal had business with this man. But to own all this...to command it!* Zaltreous thought with awed glee. *He* would first have to meet the man in charge before deciding how best to deal with him. Luckily for Zaltreous, he wasn't some defenseless simpering lord like Lapintal, he was a mage of some power, and despite the few guards he had seen so far in this palace, he knew how to handle himself in battle. After all, he had already fought against the prince himself, and five of his companions. True he had been captured, but only because he had let his guard down after being duped. It wouldn't happen again.

Flanx led them into the great room, where an ornate carpet covered the floor in front of an impressive fireplace. A fire crackled loudly, taking the chill and moisture out of the damp air as the rain continued to fall outside. In front of the mantelpiece looking into the flames, was a tall, thin stately lady dressed all in shimmery white. Her dress seemed to cling, hugging her body, yet with skirts that still flowed as she turned to face them. Zaltreous began to think he wouldn't have to overpower her, now that he knew it was a woman that had sent the invitation. A fight would be a shame really, perhaps a union would be better. He attempted a flourishing bow, and remembering his new weight too late, lost his balance and toppled unceremoniously to the floor. Politely raising a perfect hand to her rounded lips to stifle a laugh, she glanced to the guards in the corners of the room. With that one look, the men rushed forward and helped the struggling Zaltreous to his feet. Once he had been set right, they returned to their posts, and the lady in white returned the greeting with a deep graceful curtsey.

"Flanx," she almost purred in a silky voice, "go fetch us some tea, I think we shall sit for a spell."

She caught Zaltreous' eyes on that last word, and motioned for him to sit in one of the high backed chairs facing the fire. The stooped man returned almost immediately with a silver tray atop which sat cups, a tea pot, and a small pot of honey to sweeten the tea with.

"Please," she said, drawing the word out so it sounded almost smooth, "be my guest, but let's drop false appearances shall we? Though you've done commendable work with the transformation spell, I like to know who I am actually speaking to."

Shocked, Zaltreous fought down the flare of anger he felt from within from being found out when he thought he had been so cleaver. But it wouldn't do for this beauty to see him at his worst, so instead of commenting, he made a flourish with his hand and dismissed the spell on himself and Lapintal. While blue trails of sparks encircled Zaltreous where he stood, spiraling inward until he had once again taken his actual form, Lapintal fell to the floor as his flesh expanded, howling once again.

"Do get up Lapintal," The woman snapped, a cold edge to her voice, "you do bore me." Then focusing on Zaltreous once more, she eyed him up and down as he stood before her in Lapintal's baggy clothes. "An improvement," she said, "but I think this will help." With that, she snapped her fingers, and his clothes seemed to come alive. Zaltreous panicked inwardly, gritting his teeth for a moment before he realized that he himself was not being attacked. The clothing seemed to shrink around his middle, pulling closer to his skin, sleeves and pant-legs lengthening until the garments settled, fitting him precisely. He looked up at her in wonder. *She is the mage!* Not bothering to hide the flashing smile, his best smile, the one that turned him into a handsome man, he made a perfect bow, and took the closest seat.

"Much better, I think." She mused as she sat in the opposite chair, drinking in his new look. She took in that smile, his ice blue eyes, perfect slicked back black hair, and his lean physic. "Yes, I think you'll do nicely. I am called Aurastia," She commenced, speaking to the handsome man across from her before becoming distracted by shuffling sounds from behind him. She glanced down at Lapintal, who was struggling to his feet. "You can stand until I am ready for you", she commanded, and with a wave of her hand, the three hundred pound man snapped instantly to his feet and stood rigid as if lifted and bound by invisible ropes.

111

Zaltreous was impressed. "Beautiful and adept," he complimented, once again turning his brilliant smile on her.

"And you, I wonder?" she mused, raising a speculative eyebrow and tapping one red lacquered nail against her full bottom lip.

Zaltreous cocked an eyebrow, and focused his attention on the rigid Lapintal. "Fli est ira trimlabas!" *Levitate and turn upside down,* he intoned in a powerful voice as he reached a hand toward the lord. Across the room, Lapintal turned as Zaltreous' hand rotated, until he was floating above the floor with his feet pointed toward the high ceiling. The bag that had slipped from the lord's shoulder while turning now lay on the floor under the nervous man. Zaltreous left Lapintal upside down and made a new command, this time of the satchel. "Yesra ot ey!" *Come to me.* The haversack soared swiftly from its place on the carpet as if it was light as a feather, the strap barely missing a candlestick in the candelabra, as it cut a direct path through the air to his palm.

He crossed one leg, ankle over knee, and set the satchel with the *Almatraek Dim* inside, on his lap. He settled an elbow on the great pack and leaned his chin on his upturned palm, bringing him closer to her and guarding his prize jealously.

She laughed out loud, a deep throaty sound accompanied by a jovial clapping of her hands. "Ael kaiyat!" *Well done!* She declared before turning serious. "Est kel ka tay postik gol? *And what do you have there?*

Chapter 21
~ A Bigger Fish to Fry ~

The morning after the wedding, Oslan slept late. He awakened finally to the sun once again streaming through the partings between the heavy curtains of his canopy bed. Normally, Sherrod would have drawn them back long ago to awaken him unsurreptitiously, using the blasted light that would suddenly hit the prince's eyes to shock him awake. This had been one of Sherrod's subtle punishments for a lazy man, one that tried to shirk responsibilities and lay in bed all day for instance. Oslan often grumbled about this, saying that one day he would be king. If he were to have the job of making decisions; who would win out in a farmer's dispute, how much to charge for taxes, when the next wave of knights in training would be worthy of earning their dragon's fire, then he should also be able to decide for himself what time to rise. If he wanted to sleep in till noon on some occasions, so be it! That was hardly lying in bed *all* day.

But today, Oslan and Aylan had been afforded privacy and had been allowed to sleep in. Oslan stretched out as he always did before leaving his comfy warm sheets, and turned to welcome his bride into the morning. Puzzled, he looked at an empty pillow instead. *Surely, I didn't frighten my wife away after only one night!* he thought with dismay, *I was under the impression that she had enjoyed the evening's endeavours as much as I!* If he was to be honest, he had really been looking forward to many more with her. He pulled back the curtains and felt his heart leap into his throat as Sherrod stood nose to nose with him in the very spot he was about to occupy.

"Ah!" Oslan yelped, unconsciously reaching

for the sword that normally hung at his side.

"And good morning to you as well, Sire." Sherrod intoned, in a perfectly calm, and completely bored tone. It did not escape Oslan's notice that Sherrod's eye twinkled however, possibly in glee. "The new princess has risen early and bade you join her in her laboratory where she is already hard at work. You could learn from that girl you know." He pointed out, causing Oslan to roll his eyes and head for the door. "Ah-hem," Sherrod cleared his throat, forcing the prince to hesitate before leaving, and then added, "You might want to put some pants on before you do however. What colour will you have today?" And with that Sherrod turned his back to the prince and stalked over to his royal wardrobe to begin laying out the prince's clothes.

"Sherrod!" Oslan admonished.

"Well I'm sorry, Sire, but I doubt very much that your mother will be happy if she has to hire a new group of serving girls because you've scared them all away."

Oslan groaned inwardly, always hating it when he lost a battle with his man servant, which was most of the time. The man was unbearable. He decided to change the subject while he dressed. "How do you know about Aylan's workroom, did she tell you? It won't be a secret laboratory if everyone knows about it. It was supposed to be known only to us," he grumbled, feeling a little betrayed.

"Buck up young Sire," Sherrod chided as he worked, turning just long enough to give Oslan a stern look. "You should not judge your new wife in so harsh a manner. I have known about that secret passage, and all the other secret passages in this castle since before you were born."

"Wait," the prince interrupted excitedly before his servant could go on, "how many more passages?"

Sherrod finished laying out a black velvet tunic and poured the prince's wash water before answering. "Perhaps I will show you one day, if you should ever rise early enough to make the best of a full day's work!" And with that, Sherrod excused himself and slipped out of the prince's chambers, giving nothing away.

A short time later, Oslan, freshly washed, fully dressed and carrying a tray of food, held back the thick tapestry in the war room that covered the passage's entrance. He disappeared behind it, making sure that it fell back into place, and then proceeded down the hidden corridor to the room that served as Aylan's workshop.

He entered the room lined with shelves of vials, pouches and jars, never having the inclination to knock. It was his castle after all, and he felt he had the right to be anywhere at any time. Within, he found her sitting at the high table, already scrying on a town a couple of days ride away. She turned to him, distracted momentarily, and the reflection in the huge mirror shimmered and began to swirl before she focused her attention back on her spell. "Oh good, you're here," she said, all business, as he placed the tray on the table in front of her. Her tummy rumbled hungrily as the food's savoury scents reached her nose.

"Is it me, or the food that you are happier to see?" He joked, pulling her into a kiss that ruined her spell completely. Breathless, she smiled at him, but her eyes turned serious and he released her, letting her cast the spell on the mirror to scry once again. "I have found our quarry," she announced, popping a piece of bread into her mouth, and chasing it with a sip of watered wine.

The two watched in her large gilded mirror,

as their own reflection swirled, and was replaced by Entwhilen, where Aurastia and Zaltreous talked by the fire.

"Who is *she?*" Oslan asked, and was aware of the immediate glare he received from Aylan. He felt a momentary twinge of guilt at noticing the other woman's beauty while his new wife sat beside him, but it passed. After all, it wasn't Oslan's fault the woman was gorgeous, he had just happened to notice.

Zaltreous had a haversack on his lap, but as of yet, they didn't know what was inside it. Due to its size and shape though, they both felt they had a good idea. Aylan recognized that they weren't speaking the common tongue. Intently, she watched their lips move, trying to understand what was transpiring. She translated what she could for the prince, as he knew none of it. They watched the exchange, full of smiles and eyebrow raising, and Aylan leaned forward.

"Is he actually *flirting?*" She asked incredulously. Oslan merely shrugged. "This is great!" she continued, "if this woman has caught Zaltreous' eye, perhaps he will leave off trying to destroy your kingdom, after all, this whole threat began with him wanting your old mage's wife, perhaps now he will no longer care about that."

"*Our* kingdom," Oslan corrected, "and I worry that once someone is put on the path of revenge, only fulfilling it will put an end to the desire. Besides, whether he gave up or not would not force me to lose my cause. He killed the king, and I will have him locked up for the crime. Death would be simpler, but also too good for him."

The couple watched as Zaltreous pulled the book out of the satchel and reluctantly sent it through the air to the woman in white. Her eyes widened when she saw it, and reverently opened it to view the pages inside. Eventually, she closed the book and rose, carrying it back to him. She stood before him, talking, gesturing around the room, a question on her face. He looked around, then back to her, a wary kind of joy beginning to light his eyes. He asked something in return and motioned to a fat man hanging upside down.

"That's Lord Lapintal," Oslan interjected, "He inherited the title and lands in Entwhilen from his father. A great useless lump, if you ask me."

Without taking her eyes off of Zaltreous, the woman in white reached a hand out to the fat lord. He squirmed once again, mouth stretching open. Oslan heard nothing, but it was apparent that the man was screaming. Then all at once, the lord stiffened and went limp. The woman smiled at the other mage, her crimson lips saying something, pausing, talking again. Zaltreous nodded his head toward the limp form, which fell to the ground, unmoving save for a line of drool that slowly trailed to the carpet. The black haired youth that had threatened Oslan's kingdom asked the woman a question. She nodded in response and offered him her hand, which he took, bending his head to brush his lips across her knuckles. They could not see the guard's faces in the corners, but a stooped man looked on, smiling.

"I think they have made a union." Aylan said grimly, "and I also think you are down one lord."

Chapter 22
~A Message from the East~

Oslan had gathered his most trusted knights together along with other people integral to planning for a battle. The queen was present, as was Aylan, Carn, Ormond, and of course, his seer. He surveyed them now, most of them considering a map of the nearby town of Entwhilen, which was unfurled on the great table before them.

"I know this palace," Carn revealed to the group, "it is well fortified."

"We know there are hired guards there too," Aylan added, "but how many is still a mystery."

"They remain on duty day and night," confirmed Sasha, "and I have dreamed of a great battle within their walls. We will take our warriors to them."

"With a small group, we will be able to surprise them and gain entry," Ormond interjected, "I think taking a large number of troops would be a mistake. Perhaps we should have a group of cavalry at the ready though, lest something goes amiss."

"We know that the two mages have the *Almatraek Dim*. We know what some of its spells can do, but not what all of them are capable of." Oslan instructed, "By taking a large group of knights we might have more man power, however, if one of them should be affected by a spell, none of us might notice until it was too late. For all we know the mages could force our own men to fight against us, causing not only chaos, but also forcing us to hurt our own allies. I will take only my closest knights, with orders for Ormond to come after us and storm the place should we not return. This way, should one of us fall under a spell, each of us will notice the difference in personality immediately, and we will have less of our peers to watch over and protect."

"Well, I'm in!" Bowregard piped up enthusiastically as he entered the war room, followed by others from his usual party. The prince had pre-selected this group of knights to go with him, and had sent for them to come.

He filled them in on the situation and added, "We must be very careful, we can't just invade no matter how many people we have with us. She may be a noble, and even though we saw the murder, we have no proof of her crimes. We know the danger, but my subjects don't. We must keep in mind the onlookers. My family has been respected and loved for generations, which has blessed us with peaceful rule. However, if the people saw us simply manhandling nobles, they may begin to fear us and rebel. This must be handled tactfully and we must keep the casualties low in the public eye. I fear this will put us in more danger. There is no shame in staying behind should you choose to do so," Oslan assured them, "We will be up against something you may not return from."

"We will be fine." Sasha stated bluntly.

"You know this for a fact?" Queen Elsa asked, looking very relieved.

"Well, that's my opinion more so than a vision..." Sasha trailed off.

A flurry of light knocks sounded from the armoury on the other side of the door.

"Enter," allowed the queen.

A young messenger entered carrying a tiny rolled note in one hand. "It is for Prince Oslan!" the boy announced, running to place it in the prince's hand. Oslan accepted the paper and unfurled it, reading its contents.

Old friend,

I have been in contact with Aylan, and she tells me of your plight. Don't worry, she has assured me that the scrying packets within the palace are still intact, she left the grounds in order to speak with me. If you should need to do so, you need only send a bird to tell me when, then we may scry each other at the same time and talk with an added spell. Your mother, the good queen, has sent for us to attend your coronation, however, I must decline the invitation as I will be leaving Magdolyn on the morrow to go searching for the Almatraek Bright, in hopes that it may aid you. I will scry Aylan in the same place as before this evening in case you have further instructions for me.

Ever your servant,
Lazelan

"May brightness be behind you," Oslan whispered to himself. Then to the room, he said "Lazelan will go in search of the *Almatraek Bright* to aid us. He will be setting out on the morrow, and I suggest we do the same."

"Not until after the coronation!" The queen declared. "We must not put this off any longer. It will take a while for Lazelan to track this book down, so there is no rush if it is actually to be of any help."

Oslan suspected that it would take Lazelan much longer to find the book than anyone save for Aylan might realize, and he hoped to have the threat of Zaltreous finished by then. The book may be needed after though, to undo the plight of those the two mages chose not to outright kill. There was no telling what other types of harm could befall them as long as they had that evil book. To make his mother happy, Oslan decided that he would do his duty and stay long enough to have the crown placed upon his head in front of the court, making him the official king of Endalwynndale.

"Alright, mother, I will do as you ask. I suppose you must busy yourself with planning yet another feast." Then he eyed Aylan, and an angular half smile pulled up one side of his lips. He rather did enjoy seeing her look the part of a princess in beautifully tailored gowns no matter how much she hated it herself. But those were thoughts a smart husband would keep to himself. "After the coronation, we will set out for Entwhilen to recapture Zaltreous. Aylan, I suggest you speak with Lazelan before he departs, we will need his expertise on how best to defend against two mages at once."

Chapter 23
~ Marvelous Mischievousness ~

That evening, as the sun was setting on Endalwynndale, Oslan and Aylan picked their way through the bushes and ferns in the king's forest. The summer was ending, and the night was beginning to turn colder. The prince noted that Aylan had traded her summery dress in for one with longer sleeves, and had added a riding cloak for extra warmth. He preferred the cooler evening air, as the temperature suited him better while wearing thick fabrics like the velvet Sherrod had laid out for him that day. The seasons were changing now, and they were at that halfway point; too cold for summer, but much too warm yet for snow. He took a deep breath and savoured the smell and taste of the cool earthy air filling his lungs. Twigs and leaves cracked and crunched under their feet, but most of the birdsong was gone, whether it be from the time of eve, or the new coolness in the air, Oslan knew not.

They walked along the path, Oslan in the lead, looking for the spot that Aylan had previously met with Lazelan. Naturally, she had gone to a place in the forest she had been familiar with, still, Oslan hadn't liked that she had gone without him or another guard. He knew she was capable of handling herself should she come across most kinds of danger, but after seeing what had befallen her when in contact with the energy draining packets, he also knew she was not impervious to danger, whether she admitted it or not. *Stubborn woman!* He thought. Still, he wouldn't have her any other way. He actually found her strong will to be endearing.

They came to the same clearing a more

innocent Aylan had carried an orange to during a summer past in the hopes of entertaining Oslan with a game. Little had she known, the game with which she had been set up was a kissing game. Boy, had she been surprised! Still, he had rather enjoyed it.

The patch still smelled of the clove bushes that had surrounded them. Aylan pulled a hand mirror from a large pouch that hung from her belt. It was silver and had roses and briars surrounding the reflective surface. Oslan recognized it immediately as the mirror they had confiscated from Zaltreous when they had first captured him on the island. "A bit ironic, don't you think," Oslan began, "to use Zaltreous' own property to help us bring him to justice?" She smiled a wan smile, "No more than him using my magic-draining packets against me." She pointed out. "Besides, my mirror is four feet tall, I couldn't possibly be expected to lug it all the way out here, could I?" She asked sweetly. The prince snorted, knowing full well that he would have been the one to carry it. Or better yet, he could have tied it to one of the horses.

They knelt and placed the mirror on the ground under a tree where they could both sit comfortably and still see the image. Both of them were reflected back, and Aylan began to incant, "Vearta uta da Ey sechei ot isa. Vearta Lazelan." *Reveal that which I seek to see. Reveal Lazelan.* The reflection of the young couple peering into the mirror began to swirl, the rich colours of the forest bending and melding together. They faded and were replaced by an image of Lazelan seated at a table. They watched Lazelan's lips move into a broad smile at the sight of them. Aylan cast another spell, pulling the energy from her core, and Oslan found that he could hear Lazelan speaking as if he were sitting right there in the forest with them.

"-good to see you, Your Majesties." Oslan glanced at Aylan, who nodded in encouragement. "It is good to find you well, Lazelan." Oslan replied to the image within the mirror.

They talked about the new woman that Zaltreous had found for what seemed like only a short time, but Oslan became conscious of the light failing around them. Shadows of plants were growing longer, as were their own, and pretty soon they would need to use a light source to be able to find their way back.

Suddenly, Oslan heard a rustling of leaves, followed by a faint *tenk* sound as a twig fell onto the mirror's surface. The image of Lazelan began to swirl, the sound receding, as if the mage was talking to them from a great distance. Oslan supposed that the distraction was enough to snatch Aylan's attention away from her spell. He reached out and removed the twig, clearing the surface of the looking glass. He saw Aylan refocus her attention, and the picture of Lazelan solidified. Lazelan agreed that the situation was grim indeed, since as bad as he had been, Zaltreous hadn't seemed to be out to kill people. This new union of his was wrought with the ill-boding of Lapintal's quick and thoughtless death. Lazelan began to explain about a magic circlet that could be used like the packets, to weaken a mage, but unlike the packets, this had to be in contact with the person in order to affect them. If Oslan was able to obtain it and slip it onto either mage, then his band would only have to deal with magic attacks from one mage.

Tenk. Tenk, tenk. Twigs and acorns began to rain down onto the mirror, making Oslan curse in worry. These objects were hitting the mirror quite forcefully, and he feared the surface of the mirror might crack. He looked up to see what was moving around up there. *I'll put a stop to this,* the prince thought as he rose and pulled his dagger from the sheath hidden within his black leather boot. He raised the shining blade to his lips, clasping it between his teeth, and approached the trunk of the offending tree. He began to climb. The rough bark bit into his hands as his muscles strained, moving him higher and higher. He reached the lowest bough, and was able to rise onto his feet, all the while clutching a higher branch with one hand for support. There on a twig sprouting from the very branch he held, was a little person the size of a grapefruit. He wiggled an acorn back and forth, evidently trying to loosen it from the branch.

"Ah-ha!" Oslan exclaimed.

"Eep!" the creature screamed and promptly dropped out of the tree.

Below, Oslan could see it falling, with Aylan directly in its path. *Oh, this is not going to go well,* he had time to think briefly before he acted.

"Look out!" he bellowed to her, but too late. The shaggy little man landed on her head with an, "Oof!"

It was at that point that Aylan began to fuss, both screeching herself, and ruffling her hair to try to force the thing to let go and fall off. It was too bad, her hair had looked beautiful, now it was becoming a tangled mess as the little beast hung on for dear life while it flipped and flapped about with her panicked movements. Oslan sighed and began to climb down to the ground where his normally regal looking bride was currently running in circles yelling "Get it off, get it off!"

For his own part, by the time he had reached the ground, Oslan's tunic had spots where the velvet was crushed and sap clung to it in other places. Sherrod was not going to be happy about that.

Heart thumping, the prince deftly reached out both hands at once. With the left, he caught Aylan's arm to stop her from running about, and with the other, he seized the thing on her head and told it to let go. Upon closer inspection, he recognized the miniature man that yelled indignantly from his hand: "You let me go! This is undignified! I'll...I'll..."

"You'll do what, Scritch?" Oslan responded, a measure of humour in his voice. Aylan peered into the little man's eyes while making a token attempt to straighten her mussed up hair. "You again!" She accused, remembering their last encounter. "Why must you always cause trouble?"

"I'm an imp, it's in my nature! If you want to talk to a sophisticated noble, go stick your nose into your courtier-filled court!" The miniscule being grunted in a squeaky voice.

"Now, now," Oslan warned, "There's no need to be rude, you were causing trouble for us!"

"Harumph!" the imp exclaimed crossly. Aylan looked down at the mirror, which now only reflected the tops of the trees. "I'll have to wait until tomorrow to retry those spells, I don't want to drain too much of my energy." Aylan sighed, then looked to Scritch and added "now we'll have to wait to find out where this circlet is."

"Waiting's for chumps!" Scritch said pointedly, "But why bother with asking the imp? After all, he's just a forest creature, it's not like he would know anything about a circlet that baffles magic and is guarded by an evil Cyclops, nope, not Scritch!"

"Hold on a second," Oslan stopped him, "You know of this tool? What Cyclops? Cyclopes don't even exist!"

"Ha!" Scritch barked rudely, "Yeah, you're right, Cyclopes don't exist, just like little men that are only the size of a human's mug, or magic don't exist. Goodness, they'll let anyone be king, won't they?"

Oslan pointedly hung the imp upon a nearby broken branch on a smaller tree and crossed his arms across his chest. "You can stay there until you can think of something nice to say!" Oslan retorted.

"Fine, *fine*! Take me down," said the imp, trying to free himself by twisting in his little brown vest, "if you free me, I will tell you where to find the circlet." He begged.

"Oh, no. First tell me about this Cyclops and answer my questions and then you can scamper off into freedom." Oslan countered.

So the Imp told them. He explained to Aylan that a Cyclops was a giant man-like beast that had only one eye in the centre of his forehead. They were thought to be very stupid, and were very strong. He talked for a while, waiting patiently for them to ask questions, and answering the ones he could. Eventually, the prince did set Scritch free, and he disappeared underneath a nearby fern. The royal couple collected the mirror and made their way back to the castle, thinking of all the things they would need for the trip, the coronation now a far off thought.

Chapter 24
~ Scry and Scry Alike ~

"We must get there before they do!" Zaltreous cried triumphantly. He had been trying to scry Oslan's mage since their party had left Entwhilen, and had only been successful once. The one time they had managed to find Aylan, it had been fleeting, as he had felt his energy begin to drain from him for no reason he could discern, and he had been forced to end the spell lest he lose his ability to cast forever. Every mage faced this danger if his pool of energy should deplete completely. In most cases, the pool cannot recharge if there is nothing left to charge within the person's core.

Aurastia watched from her position lounging in her great armchair. She spoke luxuriantly, a bored expression on her face. "Zaltreous dear," she purred to him, "We must stay safe within these walls."

Frustrated, Zaltreous replied, fighting to keep the easily rising temper from his voice. "But Aurastia, I have read of this circlet in the book, it is very powerful. It would be advantageous to have it in our possession, and not in theirs." He walked to the great tome that now sat on a kind of pedestal across the candle lit room. By the flickering light, he began searching through the pages. Finding the spot he sought, he read the scrawled ink entry to her, excitement growing as he spoke. It was a spell for enchanting jewelry or other such things, with a notation underneath about the circlet that Oslan sought.

The circlet of Dalenden, enchanted with the power to block a mage from his or her core of energy, is a mighty artifact indeed. Mastichord, having enchanted it with the recipe above, was able to use it to overthrow several mages by sending the beautiful thing to them as a gift. By placing it on the head of someone with the power of true magic, it allowed him to drain the other mages' pools of energy, strengthening his own, with them unable to stop him.

It sits now guarded by the Cyclops Augle, an evil beast that leaves none alive that dare to enter his dark cave. It also guards itself in that any mage that tries to take it is left defenseless, cut off from his or her own pool of energy. It does not need to be worn for it to work, it only need make contact with the unfortunate mage. Without magic, no caster has lasted long, and it is said that the Cyclops sleeps lightly. Furthermore, Augle rests across the entrance to his domain, and the cave itself is guarded by wards. These wards, once triggered, disallow any kind of levitation spell, so one may not try to pass above the Cyclops while he sleeps, nor spirit the circlet away without him knowing.

"And how," began Aurastia in her languid voice, "do you propose to obtain it then? May I remind you that neither of us would be able to touch it and still cast our magic should we succeed in getting by the Cyclops. It seems like a colossal waste of time."

Zaltreous flushed, embarrassed and

frustrated that she did not agree with him. He had brought the book to her, yet he felt as though he had lost control of the situation. He found it hard to concentrate around her, like there were angry bees buzzing around in his head while he tried to think. It made him testy, unlike his usual calm and collected self. This woman was achingly beautiful, and she seemed to enjoy his company, though he hated that she saw him when he wasn't at his best.

"Don't you trust me?" He implored Aurastia to reconsider, trying hard to keep out the whiney quality that was trying hard to enter his stern voice. "If we can get the circlet, we could use it to make Oslan's mage powerless. She's just a girl, what harm could she do then?" He reasoned, not thinking of the fact that he might be insulting the woman with which he spoke. To Zaltreous, it was true though, Aylan was just a measly girl. When he had first seen her, she had been nothing but a gangly, awkward child with freckles. Whereas Aurastia...well, let's just say she was clearly more mature, sophisticated. "We could own this kingdom you and I, no one would be able to stop us!" He threw out hopefully.

"We needn't travel at all," she argued, "we have the spell right here, we can simply enchant something I already possess and use it."

"That might work, Aurastia," he said pointedly, "except for the fact that there is a slight snag in that idea. The recipe calls for the blood of the spell caster's own first born child, and unless there is something you haven't told me, we are both unable to come up with that necessary ingredient. Creating our own copy also wouldn't prevent Oslan from getting the power of the existing circlet." He reasoned. "There is a simple solution to this problem though. We will go to the cave, and your servant, Flanx, can go in after it!"

From where he stood unobtrusively against the wall, Flanx started. Zaltreous saw the puny servant's face blanch before Aurastia was on her feet, gracefully gliding across the room until she had put herself between them.

"Zaltreous, you are forgetting something, quite a few things, actually, not the least of which is that Flanx would be completely defenseless against a Cyclops, and I rather do enjoy his service."

From the corner of his eye, Zaltreous saw the old man visibly relax, and heard him mumble a dry "Thank you, Milady", accompanied by a slight bow. *Coward!* The impatient Zaltreous thought.

"We should stay here where it is safe, Zaltreous. If they are successful in their quest for the circlet, my fortress will save us, its walls are all but impregnable. They won't be able to get in to place it on either of our heads." Aurastia pointed out, "Besides my dear, even though they go to fetch it, there is no guarantee of their success. The Cyclops may kill them all in his fury of being robbed, and may take care of Oslan for you."

Zaltreous felt his body tense, his stomach tightening. "No!" he whispered as the realization dawned on him that he might not be able to exact his revenge. "I can't have come this far to have my victory taken away from me by such a creature!" He looked at Aurastia, the image of the flames from the fireplace dancing across his eyes, a new resolve in his voice. "Stay here then where it is safe," he cried spitefully, "I will go with Flanx and we will retrieve the treasure without you. I will be taking the book with me, perhaps it has something else inside that will help us."

Flanx shook his head in denial, as in anger, Zaltreous made a move to slam the book shut on its pedestal and began to buckle the leather straps that would hold it closed against the elements.

Panicked, Aurastia did the only thing she could think of to keep the priceless book within her walls. She rushed to Zaltreous, and running her fingers up into his perfect black hair, she held him fast, kissing him deeply.

Chapter 25
~ A Party ~

Oslan wanted to join in the hunt for Zaltreous, but both Aylan and the queen mother were in agreement for once, that he should stay put at the palace. "This kingdom has already lost a king," Elsa begged him to see reason, "do not let it lose another before you are yet crowned." Aylan took a more direct approach. "Oslan," she said softly, taking both of his hands in hers, and stepping close enough that he could smell the sweet scent of lilacs on the air around her, "Without the *Almatraek Bright*, I have no way of fending off whatever spell he puts you under. As long as he has the *Almatraek Dim*, you are safer where he can't see you. I have already checked on the packets we created after the last tournament to make sure they are still secure. They will continue to shield anyone in the palace from being scried."

But Oslan would not consent to staying within the castle walls, even when Ormond offered to return to provide him with regular reports on any news they had found on Zaltreous' whereabouts. "I know you worry for my safety," Oslan responded, making sure to glance around the room, looking all present in the eye before finally returning his gaze to Aylan. "That is why I intend on having Carn and yourself," he said with a squeeze to Aylan's hands, "to watch over me directly. I ask you to remember that the *Almatraek Dim* was sought after for years before it surfaced the last time. I can't be kept in the castle like a bird in a cage until it surfaces again.

We know he is holed up in a fortress, which means he is likely under the wing of a treacherous noble. I believe in this we have an advantage. My coronation gives us the perfect guise to seek out the traitor and see what we're up against. All nobles will receive an invitation to bear witness as I take the throne, this particular one we shall deliver by hand."

"But Oslan," Ormond responded immediately, "What if Zaltreous sees you coming and rallies an attack then and there?"

The prince sighed heavily, searching his heart for a way to make them understand. "Whatever comes to pass, I need to be out there protecting my people as much as they would want me to be protected. We have already conquered Zaltreous once, and we will do it again." The prince surveyed the room. "My knights and mage are skilled, and if it came down to it, it would be a fight of many against one."

"Two," Aylan corrected, "the noble also appears to be a mage, which is why we need the circlet before we try anything as foolhardy as this."

"I'm not looking for a fight, only information," the prince replied tiredly, "the circlet will have to wait until after the coronation, I know that, and I'm not crazy. I do not wish a fight until we are ready for one."

"But you're the crown prince, they will recognize you. What is your plan then? Simply tell them 'no sorry, I can't fight you right now, we're not ready to defeat you'? What do you expect their response to be to that? 'Oh no worries, why don't you all go limber up and we'll have a nice battle when you're ready.' Come on Oslan, see reason!" His mother interjected.

"They won't be able to recognize me if I am not the one holding the envelope," he said pointedly.

They argued and argued, but in the end, Oslan wouldn't be put off. Oslan, Aylan and Carn decided to call on some of the other knights that had been brave enough to band together against Zaltreous in the past. They had been sending messages by wing, and the men were honoured to have the prince fight by their side.

Thornton was eager to have the prince join them, as was a heavy-set teenager called Trembleton. This boy was as tall and as wide as a bear, and at thirteen, continued to grow. His red hair frizzed out in tight curls around his head in contrast to the straight haired, Bowregard. Bow's hair was almost the same shade of red, if not a bit darker, but where Trembleton's resembled an out of control bird's nest, Bowregard's lay in a neat loose coif to the ears. Bow was as tall as Trembleton, making them both a full head taller than Thornton, but where Trembleton bore a heavy sort of weight around his middle, Bow sported pure muscle.

These boys had all trained with Oslan under Carn since boyhood, and when Oslan began to work one-on-one with Ormond as his skill with a sword grew, the prince never let himself forget his friends. Oslan looked once again at the curled piece of parchment he held in his gloved hand. It was a note that had come by bird from Bow. It suggested that they meet at a tavern in a nearby village in four days' time. Oslan had sent a reply by pigeon upon receipt of the note, and it was time for his trio at the palace to ride to meet them. Oslan and Carn took the stairs down the tower to the hall of the East wing of the keep. They moved toward the upper hallway's main staircase that would take them to the front doors where a stable boy would meet them with three horses for their ride.

As Oslan and Carn rounded the corner of the keep's upper banister, they could see Aylan waiting for them below, but she wasn't alone. Both she and Sasha wore thicker gowns than normal, and Sasha sported a riding cloak for protection from weather and dust on the road. Aylan wore the blue velvet cloak with stars that shone along the trim that she had worn the last time they had encountered the evil mage. It had been a gift from the kingdom's former mage, and Oslan knew that it was protected by spells that would act as a shield even against sword or magic, as long as the cloak remained closed around her. As the men descended the last set of stairs, Sasha took a step towards them.

"I know you weren't counting on my company," Sasha began in her ringing voice, "but Millie practically forced me into a travelling cloak, all the while begging that I let you know if any harm would befall Bowregard."

"She is really quite taken with him, you know," put in Aylan.

"They are both quite smitten with each other," Sasha added sagely. "In fact, I would not at all be surprised if theirs was to be the marriage that will come next in this kingdom."

Oslan's ears burned with the mention of his wedding, and though he had not been nervous about the ceremony or joining himself to Aylan, he had felt afraid lest he should ever fall short as a husband. Now he was be responsible for her life, above the lives of everyone in the kingdom, *his* kingdom. "Have you set her up with packets for her protection?" Oslan asked Aylan. *I hope she thought to make some of those pills that turn a person invisible,* he thought, *those might come in handy.*

Sasha pulled back her cloak showing a fat purse hanging from her sturdy leather belt. "Yes, she did, though I argued against it." Sasha confirmed.

"Why would you do such a thing?" Oslan questioned, "You should be able to defend yourself, and you carry no other weapons."

"I only had time to make one batch of packets, Oslan," Aylan confided, "It was either those, or packets to stop Zaltreous from being able to scry us. I couldn't make both, and I dare not remove them from the palace where he could gain control of your family."

Oslan nodded in acknowledgement and grimly ordered, "Let's go."

Chapter 26
~ Almad Spurr ~

Two days later, the four weary riders from Endalwynndale rode between the first tall wooden houses of a town called Entwhilen. After a hard ride that afternoon to make it to the town before dusk, they were dust covered from the road and wanting nothing more than to find their friends and a sleeping pallet for the night.

Sasha spotted the stables first, and after watching the gleam in the eyes of the stable boy when he caught the gold glint of the coin Oslan threw to him for his work, they made their way on foot to a tavern called the Elder Bear. Boisterous laughter poured out in loud waves from the windows, which spilled sound and warm light into the streets.

Carn opened the door for the ladies to enter. Immediately, like a rainstorm washing away mud from a cart-wheel, relief washed away any concern Oslan had felt about finding their friends. There sat Thorn, Bowregard and Trembleton enjoying a drink at the bar while a bard dressed in strange fashion told stories of an adventure at sea to anyone that would listen. Many people were intent on the tale, and only a few turned their heads as they took notice of the group coming through the collection of revellers.

As Oslan's group made their way to their companions, he took in the room. The torches burning on the walls made this place fairly well lit compared to other taverns he had visited. He liked that. It made it easier to see the intentions sometimes hidden on a man's face. To his left, a long slightly rounded bar took up most of the space until it connected to a wall that hid the kitchen. The sound of clanging pots came to him, and the smell of roasting meat and strong ale made his mouth water. Along the back wall there was a staircase to a second floor. It was possible that this tavern was an inn as well, perhaps his friends would not have to travel any further to find a room. With the size of this gathering, the rooms might all be taken, but Oslan took for granted that some poor souls would be ousted if the proprietor found that he could be serving the prince. Reaching his friends, his greeting was almost lost to great shouts of appreciation and applause as the bard took a bow and sat to take in a drink before beginning his next story.

With a grin and a nod to the newly arrived prince, Thorn bounded off through the mob to the place where the bard had been performing his recitation. Oslan now saw that the floor was raised in a space big enough to seat two full tables, but if any usually sat there, they had been removed for this occasion. Performers were useful to inn keepers and tavern owners alike, as they often drew in a crowd which meant more business for them. People loved listening to bards for entertainment. They could hear of far-off places that they would never dare travel to on their own, and be taken away from ordinary life with dangerous tales or stories of love. Bards also helped to pass the news from one town to the next, so for all this, they were often given a room and meals for free as well as their pay in exchange for their services.

After a brief word and a toothless grin from the white bearded performer, Thornton took up the attention of the patrons of the tavern by presenting his lute and beginning to strum a few chords. The din of conversations that had begun when the bard left the stage calmed until Thorn's voice could be heard clearly above the remaining low conversation and glasses clinking.

Though he was a lithe boy, barely half the size of other patrons at the tavern, his voice filled the room easily as it took on a projected quality that commanded attention. His words rang out: "My name is Thornton Longshot, bowman and singer extraordinaire! Let me share a little light with you on this darkening eve!"

At the bar, Bowregard and Trembleton met with their newly arrived party and left the stools to get a table with proper chairs closer to the stage. At Thorn's introduction, they clapped and cheered relentlessly, with many a tipsy man and woman around them joining in enthusiastically. *They don't even know what is coming!* Thought Oslan, as he marked their eagerness, *it's amazing what a little drink and a group mentality can accomplish.* Thorn began to strum and sing:

"'T'was on an evening quite like this,
The darkness rolling in,
That Almad Spurr arrived in town,
Upon his face, a grin,
He made his way into a pub,
This very Elder Bear,
He found a seat beside the bar,
And spotted golden hair.

The lass was small, the barkeep's aid,
And he, a Dwarven lad,
With reddish hair and full blown beard,
Charisma not too bad,
He sidled up to the barkeep's side,
An order for to make,
And pinched the rump of the serving girl,
A most grievous mistake.

The Halfling wench threw down her tray,

The crowd made her some room,
"You've picked the wrong one to accost,"
She cried, and seized a broom,
The mugs were swept up into hands,
As she leapt upon the bar,
But Almad laughed into her face,
As she prepared to spar.

A crowd drew round to see the row,
Exciting this would be,
And wagers passed from lip to lip,
When broom-tip whacked Spurr's knee,
He yowled as though he hit the roof,
A goose-bump on his leg,
And used the pause to take a sip
Right from the barkeep's keg.

He stood up tall, his wobble small,
And still he showed no fear
He went for her, but slipped and fell,
Through puddles made of beer,
Spurr went down hard between two stools,
Reached out with flailing hand,
He caught her foot, she tumbled too,
And upon him she did land.

She tried to roll clear of the fool,
He held her in his grasp,
Saying "Sorry, I'd no right to pinch."
She yelled "With me, you ask!"
And so he looked deep into eyes
As stormy as the sea,
And said "Then dear I ask for you
To plant a kiss on me!"

She looked at all the men drawn 'round,
And Almad let her go,
She helped him up and checked his knee,

141

Of that she made a show,
When all had laughed and then returned
To the solace of his drink,
She laid on Spurr a kiss so deep,
The poor man couldn't think.

After that it seemed that our old dog
Learned a new trick,
For he asked the blonde again for kisses
In an accent thick,
She eyed the bar and sighed "I can't,
I've work here, I suppose."
He cried "Don't leave me hanging here,
I'm ready to propose!"

The folks that filled the Elder Bear on this night reacted around Oslan as if they were there, witnessing the events in Thorn's song. They cheered when the serving girl hit Spurr with the broom, and seemed to collectively sigh as they shared their kiss. A pleasantly rounded barmaid pushed her way through the gathered throng, stopping a foot from Thornton.

"You're kind of small," she bellowed, "Are you this Almad Spurr that you sing of?"

The group crowed in laughter as Thornton went red to the tips of his hair, and shook his head vehemently *no*. Oslan's and Carn's low chuckles joined the rest. *This is quite possibly the first time Thornton has been embarrassed on stage,* Oslan remarked to himself jovially.

"Good then," cried the bar wench, "*You* don't have to *ask*!"   And with that, to the surprise of all those gathered at the bar, but astonishing no one more than Thorn himself, she threw herself upon him and kissed him deeply enough that it was fit for its own song.   A cheer rose up in the bar as everyone watched the youth first struggle, then succumb to the wild embrace.

"When you are finished kissing my friend," Bow said from his seat beside the woman, in a low voice that only she would hear, "The prince of Endalwynndale would like to order a meal."

Her startled eyes flew open, and she hastily ended the kiss.   No matter how cute a bard was, money from a prince was better.

"Take heed," Bow warned her, "no one is to know.   We are merely soldiers out for a night on the town."   She nodded excitedly, "Whatever you say, sir.   Now let me get you all some supper."

With heavily-lidded eyes, dishevelled hair and a crooked grin, Thorn rejoined them and sat at the table.

That night passed pleasantly, filled with hot food and cool drink.   After a few more hours of entertainment despite their weariness, the travellers from Endalwynndale finally stumbled into beds above the tavern at a very late hour.

Chapter 27
~ Tipsy Tip ~

Oslan awoke to the light clacking of Carn donning his armour, and the other knights' snores. They sounded like a storm, all crackling lightning and booming thunder.

"Good day, your highness." Carn's voice boomed the moment the prince opened his eyes. In response, the sawing snores stopped with a snort, and Thorn reflexively pulled a pillow over his head to block out the sound in his half asleep state. Oslan screwed his eyes shut against the cold light and tried to unstick his tongue from the roof of his mouth. He grumbled about why Carn had to speak so loudly first thing in the morning.

Carn's chuckle was a loud rumble, and it seemed to Oslan that although his knight didn't seem to be doing anything differently than usual to strap on his armour, he was definitely not making any move to dampen the sharp sound of metal on metal as he moved. Trembleton groaned and started to stir, moving his large form gingerly. Thorn finally lifted one side of the pillow from his head long enough to ask Carn if he was planning on alerting Zaltreous of their whereabouts with all the racket. Bow's groggy response of "If he did attack it would probably hurt less," came from behind covers pulled up over his head.

The prince had never noticed how painful the sound of armour could be, usually he welcomed it, but this morning it felt as though the sharp sound was driving its way to the very middle of his head. Fuzzily, Oslan remembered the bar maid the night before repeatedly bringing over mugs of ale sent by the proprietor, herself, and many a young lady that hovered around the table to meet Thorn. After the first couple of drinks, Thorn had started to insist that his friends take the ale and mead instead.

Now, they were all paying the price with mouths that tasted dry and stale, stomachs that felt vial, and headaches that seemed to encompass the world. All except Carn of course, who had flatly refused any drinks beyond the first two mugs. Oslan's heart was warmed by the man who was slated to protect him for taking that duty so seriously, and always ensuring that he would be of sound mind, unclouded by drink. He also felt a twinge of jealousy over the fact that the slightest noise wasn't making Carn cringe like the rest of them. He made a mental note to stick to the same two mug limit as Carn did.

His thoughts turned to Aylan as he laid still taking solace from the warmth provided by his covers. He wondered how the ladies in their room next door were faring. He couldn't remember if they had shared in the ale or not. If not, no doubt that today they would show no mercy in throwing jibes at the men. They would be insufferable. Still, he did not wish on them the sour feeling he had now. With a sigh, he threw back his blanket and sat up. The world lurched around him as his head spun. This was going to be a long day.

Carn left the younger men to nurse their bellies and headaches as they slowly dressed, and he went to collect the ladies before heading downstairs. Knocking lightly on the door, he waited for a response that did not come. Feeling somewhat like an intruder, he listened briefly at the door for the sound of voices. When none came, he decided to continue downstairs to investigate what passed as breakfast in the tavern below. His heavy boots clunked on the wooden steps as he slowly took them one at a time. The room below came into view, and soft snatches of conversation and the rich smells of cooking reached his senses. His mouth watered at the familiar smell of bacon, as he surveyed the tables of people to find the ladies he sought. He was surprised to see how busy the place was. This was a welcome sight, and meant that the tavern was a well-liked spot for eating a hearty first meal of the day. He heard Sasha's musical voice calling his name, and he scanned the room in that direction, finding the ladies seated by the back wall across the dining hall by the warmly lit fireplace. They had chosen a table that would accommodate them all once the other men were up and about.

A dark skinned stranger in a cloak and hood that almost completely hid his face was sitting to their left. Each Lady was calmly sipping from a hot cup, and a third ale-filled mug and plate laden with food was steaming in front of the man. Alarmed at the stranger's presence, Carn instinctively reached for his blade. With an almost imperceptible shake of her head, Aylan warned against his reaction and his hand slowly drew away. Carn quickly closed the gap between them, and the man started, poised with some ham on his knife, halfway to his mouth. He brandished it at the knight, meat and all, and the ladies raised their hands in protection from the juices being flung in their direction.

"It is alright," Aylan soothed, "This is Sir Carn, and he is with us. He wishes you no harm."

"Indeed, why don't you continue with your meal, and your tale?" Sasha finished.

The man looked sideways at the two ladies, and put an arm protectively around his breakfast before taking a drink. To Carn, the man smelled as if he had been drinking all night, and looked none the steadier for it. The stranger twisted the knife toward himself to pop the juicy meat into his mouth.

As the hooded man chewed, Carn sat, keeping a short distance between them, and looked around for the serving girl. He spotted her laying mugs on another table, already looking in their direction. She finished with her other customers and rushed over. The flush that rose on her cheeks nearly touched the heavy bags under her eyes from a late night and early rising. "What can I get for you, and will Sir Thornton be joining you this morning?" She breathed, obviously eager to see him again.

"He will be along shortly, I am sure," Carn replied, "and will probably enjoy a brew for his head and a plate for his belly. Please bring enough for five."

"Make it seven!" Aylan piped up. With an embarrassed blush of her own for her eagerness, she explained "We were waiting for you gentlemen to join us, but we have been awake long, and my stomach is beginning to pain me for not having eaten." The serving girl nodded and left to see to their meal.

In a slurred deep voice, the man started talking, forming the words around the food still in his mouth. "Like I said, this Zaltreous, did you say his name was?" He took the opportunity to spear another chunk of meat while he waited for confirmation from the ladies before going on, wetly talking around his new bite. "I saw him with it at the butcher's shop. He was obviously trying to keep it hidden, but with a book that big, people are going to notice it no matter what you do to try to keep it a secret. He was acting like he thought everyone in the place was going to try to steal it. I mean come on mate, it's only a book, and half the town can't even read!"

He popped another piece of his breakfast into his mouth and his face lit up like he had just made a discovery, his chewing slowing as his thoughts raced. "Say, you don't think that book of his was worth something do you? It wasn't a very practical size to read. In fact, the only time I've ever seen a book that big was when a man and his followers came to town preaching out of some holy book. That book was almost as big as the one this Zaltreous had. I bet that's what it was! Are you followers of this Zaltreous? I wonder why he didn't stop to preach. He saw our Lord Lapintal, and they went off in the same direction from there. Will he be preaching today do you think?"

As the questions came, Aylan reached into a pouch at her side. She bumped Sasha under the table, who took the cue and pointed across the room away from Aylan. "Hey," she exclaimed, "Is that him there?" The stranger turned his head to follow where she pointed, somewhat excited, but his face fell almost immediately. Aylan took the opportunity to sprinkle the powder she held in her fingertips over his food while he was distracted.

"No, no, weren't you listening?" He scolded Sasha as he blindly speared another piece of his meal, "I said he had black hair, that fellow's hair is dark brown at best." Sasha let a look of disappointment cloud her beautiful features before sighing. Carn caught sight of the prince and knights descending the stairs.

"Well my good man, thank you for your help." Carn interjected.

"It's too bad that we couldn't help you find who you were looking for." Aylan added quickly. "Perhaps if you sit at the table by the door, you'll be able to see her better when she enters." She gestured to an empty table by the door.

"Good idea!" The man said cheerfully. He promptly got up and Carn stood. The man carried his heavy tray of food to the empty table, and sat so he had the best vantage point of the people coming in.

"That was strange." Carn remarked under his breath as he sat again.

"The powder I put into his food will make him forget us and the conversation he had with us. Or rather, we won't seem important enough to mention to anyone else. The only thing his mind will focus on is the idea we just implanted. He will look for a girl either until he finds one that he has conjured in his own mind, or until the powder wears off, long after we've gone in a couple of hours.

Chapter 28
~ Summarizing a Summons ~

Oslan, Trembleton, Thornton and Bow had no sooner sat down at the table when the serving girl arrived carrying all of their plates in two loads. The smells of bacon and ham and trotters surrounded them, and Oslan's mouth began to water in anticipation of the first bite.

"Good morning Thornton," she purred in greeting, "Oh, and your Majesty, of course." She added in a hasty whisper before making an awkward curtsey and then returned to the kitchen for their tisane.

"I think someone was waiting for you," Trembleton teased, "That must have been some kiss!"

Eyes wide, staring at the heaping plate of pork in front of them, Thorn replied in delight: "Aye, but now my friends it is time that I bring something even sweeter to my lips!"

"How did we come by such a hearty meal so early in the day?" Trembleton questioned Carn, but it was Bow that answered:

"This is the Elder Bear, it's famous for serving pork at every hour of the day and night. That is how they draw their crowd."

"Eat up," Carn advised, "The greasy parts will help to settle your stomach."

"That, or the tea will." Aylan added pointedly between delicate bites.

With a look that told Carn that he didn't necessarily believe what the knight professed, Oslan reached for a piece of bacon and gingerly bit off a piece. He chewed slowly and swallowed, feeling the greasy pulp slide down his throat. His stomach gave an uncomfortable lurch. He forced himself to consume more, knowing that his body needed the nourishment. As he ate, the rolling sensation inside his stomach began to calm.

"It might just be me," he said to the others that had not yet dared food, "but I do believe I'm starting to feel a trifle better."

"See, what did I tell you?" Carn interjected and barked a laugh while slapping Oslan's shoulder, a habit he was prone to do. Normally Oslan didn't mind it, but the sharp sound on his armour so close to his ears while he was in this state made his head ring. He winced with the explosion of pain.

"Well what do you expect? You haven't even tried your tea yet." Aylan pointed out smugly. "You brought this on yourself, you know."

Oslan groaned again. "I knew it," he said almost under his breath, "insufferable."

Aylan harrumphed and went back to her breakfast, making a point to sip some tea as she did. "Mmm, it's delicious," she declared.

Oslan sighed and picked up his own mug, and bringing it to his lips, found that the smell of meat that they had all been enjoying was now overcome by the scents of sweet plants. He ventured a sip, and the aroma he had just smelled seemed to come alive on his tongue in rich, mingling sensations. He swallowed, and his jaw went slack as he realized in shock that his headache was actually lessening.

"What's wrong?" Trembleton asked immediately.

"Nothing," the prince replied quickly, "Just drink the tea."

The young knights all reached for their mugs and started to down the hot liquid. Carn and Aylan shared a knowing look and a smile.

After they had eaten their fill, the party rose,

and paid the barkeep well. After copious compliments about the food, they made their way between the tables toward the door that was now propped open to allow the morning light and fresh air to enter. As they passed the last table, the cloaked stranger reached out and snagged Oslan's arm. In a second, Carn's hand was on his sword hilt, and Oslan's was on his knight's arm, stopping him from drawing his weapon. Almost as if seeing them for the first time, the man enquired: "You haven't seen a girl have you? She's short and round and she don't put up with foul language, I can tell you that!" Oslan looked around the tavern and merely shook his head in the negative. The man released him. "That's alright," he sighed, "She's bound to come around shortly. Say, would you lot mind moving, you're blocking my view of the door?"

With that, Oslan led the party into the streets that were slowly coming alive. The odd merchant walked to work, making ready to open their businesses for the day. "What was with the crazy guy inside? Do you think he sits there every day looking for his long lost love or something? Does he really think she'll come?" Trembleton asked, always without tact.

"He wasn't crazy," Aylan explained, "he was under our influence. Sasha had a vision last night that the man might know the whereabouts of Zaltreous, and he did."

"What? Tell me you didn't just walk up to him and ask: 'Excuse me, but you haven't happened to have seen any evil mages lurking about have you?'" Bowregard asked, truly interested.

"No," Sasha replied, "but we rose early, and he, just waking from a night of sleeping with his head on the table, looked even more worse for wear than you."

"We simply offered him some tea for his head, some pork for his belly, and he was eager to talk to two ladies visiting from a distant land."

Thorn snorted, "Endalwynndale is hardly distant." He pointed out.

"True, but he needn't have known where we actually came from." Sasha finished emphatically.

They walked on until they came to a shop that was already opened for business. Carn's plan was to casually start up a conversation with the shopkeeper, asking the whereabouts of this Lord Lapintal. Aylan was to pose as a Lady who had a meeting with the fat man. Carn was going to pose as her hired guard that had simply gotten them lost. Any shopkeeper would know where the lord's manor houses were simply from making deliveries, and would be eager to help. After all, if the guard mentioned that a certain shop keeper had helped him find his way so his lady could conduct important business, the lord might pay the store a visit to thank him.

As it turned out, the manor house was empty. Bow picked up the trail of wagon wheels eerily without hoof tracks to accompany them. It looked as though they were in for a long day of tracking.

Chapter 29
~ An Invitation ~

The next day, though sunny, brought with it a chill to the air, and Flanx noted that he could see the breath of the messenger that held an envelope for his mistress. The bent white-haired man held out his hand to accept the envelope, but the boy standing before him refused to hand it over.

"I was instructed to place this only in the hands of the lady of the house!" Thorn trembled, now without his lute or bow. Flanx sighed at the pomp and circumstance surrounding the message, and bade him to follow. Thorn dutifully carried it through the house to where Aurastia and Zaltreous sat eating breakfast and planning defenses against Oslan's forces. Aurastia's foremost guard and impeccable marksman, Cafernaght, who was unwelcome to eat with them, yet whose presence was required for the planning, stood behind them offering his input.

"I have been training the lads with their bows, and they are becoming quite formidable," he was saying in his deep, gruff voice, "In fact, I believe that our arrow slits will be our greatest advantage."

Zaltreous noted that Aurastia's countenance seemed to brighten slightly as Flanx entered the room. Zaltreous scowled at the man. He had to admit that Flanx was a good servant, but he barely ever left them alone, making Zaltreous feel like he had no privacy within the small castle. He always felt that he was under the shriveled man's scrutiny, and it made him hold his tongue from telling Aurastia his innermost thoughts, lest he be overheard. His mother had warned him once that servants were like well-behaved children; when silent, they could blend into the scenery, and be easily forgotten, but it was best not to forget that they still had ears.

Flanx presented Aurastia as the one the message was meant for, and Thorn placed the envelope in her hand. He stepped back to wait for her reply,   and Flanx moved to stand against the wall in his customary at-the-ready manner. Zaltreous watched, curiosity making him itch, as Aurastia stared at the fine paper of the envelope for a moment before breaking the wax seal. Her dark eyes skimmed the page for what seemed like an eternity.   "It is an invitation to the prince's coronation. I am to be the chalice bearer." She finally said. Zaltreous started to laugh.

"Surely, you're not going!" He reasoned.

"Actually, I think it will be a wonderful opportunity to see this other mage for myself." She retorted gently.

"But what about staying safe within the walls?" Zaltreous asked incredulously, doing a halfway fine impersonation of her.

"They can't do anything to me in open court, Zaltreous," she pointed out. "You, they could arrest on sight, but I am a noble that they have no qualms with. As a baroness within a rational riding distance, I am required to attend to be part of the court that will witness his ascension to the throne. We all must play our part." Turning to Thorn, she said "you may tell your master that I wouldn't miss it for the world."

Thorn bowed his acknowledgement and quitted the room, hurrying back through the castle to his freedom. As he passed through a room with a large fireplace, he noticed a large book on a pedestal. *That's it, the Almatraek Dim! I could grab the book and be off with it before anybody noticed!* he thought.   He looked around, and seeing no guards, he took a tentative step forward. A voice close behind him almost made him jump out of his skin.

"The door is this way."

Thorn turned, heart beating hard in his chest. "Of, of course," he stammered to the old man that had met him at the door. Fearing that he may be detained there, he made a b-line for the door. Flanx shook his head in annoyance and returned to the great room where the two mages were still bickering over the matter of Aurastia's visit to the capital.

"But, you will be walking right into their hands," Zaltreous began to protest. Aurastia cut him off, trying to sooth his stinging ego. "No arguments Zaltreous, I will be going. You are a brilliant and strong mage," she complimented, "but since you have never been one, you forget there are things required of a noble. The lack of my presence would alert them to something being wrong, and we don't need that kind of attention before we are ready for them. Since you must stay here, I will grant you access to my workroom. Flanx can be most helpful in finding my various ingredients and potions, and he will be more than happy, I'm sure, to help you find your way around." Zaltreous grudgingly acquiesced, not looking forward to being stuck in this place with Flanx, but without her. He was beginning to lose his appetite. Then an idea occurred to him.

"Perhaps you should take Flanx with you, just for safety's sake. I cannot scry to keep an eye on you, as they have taken liberties to prevent it. But perhaps Flanx will find a way to fix that problem while you are mingling with the other courtiers."

He felt his heart leap into his throat as she took a moment to study his face and gaze into his eyes. He wanted to squirm in his chair, feeling like a child being scrutinized for causing trouble, but he resisted, holding fast to his calm demeanor. How did she manage to make him feel so powerless? "Fine." She assented after a long pause, dragging out the word like a fisherman letting out his line. He secretly wondered if she saw him as the fish, or the worm.

Within the hour, the servants had Aurastia's things prepared, and the sable carriage pulled noisily away from the great manor. Zaltreous felt his shoulders relax as they disappeared through the gate, leaving him as master of the house in their absence. He made his way to her workroom, and for the first time, slowly pushed open the door. The room was brightly lit, with three large windows set into one long wall opposite the door. The cold white light of the fall sun streamed in, shedding a considerable amount of light on the book titles that lined four book cases opposite them. The room was long and skinny, with wooden shelves at either end containing vials of liquids and small wooden boxes that contained things that the dark only knew.

In the centre of the room was a sturdy wooden table, long like the room, with an apparatus for holding rows of vials, a small caldron, and a sooty metal bowl meant for holding a small fire, should a concoction need to be heated from below. There was a chill in the room, but a warmth in his blood at his excitement held back the cold. Zaltreous set to work looking through the things now at his disposal, starting with setting a fire in the bowl for an added bit of heat.

He bellowed for a servant to prepare some food, and a while later, he was enjoying a meal of hot chicken, wine, and root vegetables. He looked through a book he had found on the shelf, noting that this was decidedly not Aurastia's handwriting. It was too scratchy, and lacked the gentle loops from

157

her earlier note to him. In fact, Zaltreous could almost swear that it was a man's writing, and he wondered if she was in the practice of dictating while her favourite servant wrote down her findings. He wasn't sure he would trust a servant to handle such delicate notes. Some spells were so finicky, that a drop too many or too less would ruin a whole concoction. Although, she seemed to depend on Flanx for a lot of things, too many things, he thought jealously.

He summoned a servant to bring him a bowl of water, not knowing if she normally allowed them to enter into her domain. She wasn't here though, and he was the man of the house. He took the liberty to make these trifling decisions in her absence. What's the worst that could happen, he reasoned. The servant came in with the bowl, and stood, holding it nervously. "Well, what are you waiting for? Put it on the table!" Zaltreous whispered dangerously. The servant shuffled his feet, but made no move closer to Zaltreous. Frightened, he explained, speaking quickly with his eyes plastered on the ground. "I'm sorry, Master Zaltreous, but Aurastia would have us flogged if we put anything that could spill near her beloved books." Cringing, he went on, "She never takes food or drink in here, lest something serious should happen. Some of her books are irreplaceable."

"You are dismissed then," Zaltreous said quietly, seething inside. Even without her here, her power overshadowed his. "After you bring me the bowl of water, of course." The servant edged slowly closer to Zaltreous, his face pulled back in fear, his head turning toward the side like a dog preparing to be beaten. The slap was a verbal one though. As the servant handed the mage the bowl, Zaltreous gave one more order to the cringing man. "Come back with a cup of milk."

The servant paled, and for a moment, Zaltreous was actually afraid that the man might faint. Instead, the servant scurried out as quickly as a mouse avoiding a cat.

Zaltreous placed the bowl above the book he was reading on the table. With this water, he would intermittently attempt to scry the palace, to see if Flanx had granted him the ability to see through whatever wards the young mage had placed there. If the old man was successful in thwarting a mage's spell, perhaps he would be a good scribe after all. It gave Zaltreous more food for thought about how he wanted to run the kingdom once it was his. His and Aurastia's, of course, if she would have him. If not, he thought dangerously, perhaps he would have her pretty little head, and gain her valuable servant.

Chapter 30
~ Chalice Bearer ~

"We can probably skip the coronation completely!" Aylan cried dramatically, "Because when your mother finds out what you've done, she will kill you!"

Aylan and Oslan were in the chambers that they now shared, preparing for the coronation that would begin in a short while. They had just gone over what the procession would look like, who was to do what, and when, and the room had become empty for the first time all morning, giving the couple a moment of privacy.

Oslan had wisely kept from his mother and Aylan the fact that he had specifically requested Aurastia as his chalice bearer, a station that would put her into proximity close to him and the wine he was to consume. Inwardly, Oslan was not worried. He knew that Aylan would be by his side to protect him, as well as hundreds of guards at the palace. This unknown baroness wouldn't dare try anything. If she did, she would never make it out alive.

"It's not in her best interest to cause trouble today." He reasoned calmly, "If she did, we would publically have a reason to imprison her." Considering it, he added "It would actually be to our advantage if she did try to harm me. Perhaps you can goad her a little."

He watched in good humour as Aylan began to go crimson in frustration, sputtering. "What? No! I will not! Could not! Do you not care for your own safety? Would you make me a widow already?"

She wheeled in exasperation, threw her hands in the air and stalked off toward their inner chamber where her clothes were laid out for the ceremony.

Inwardly, he smirked. He knew she was worried about him, but he had complete faith in her abilities to protect him. Right now, he was just enjoying the show of her emotions. It proved to him how much she cared for him, and he was fairly certain that he had miraculously won this round. She only threw up her hands and walked away when she was giving up. It was a good sign. His heart soared. He did love it when a good plan came to a head.

There was a knock at the door, and then the room was full once again with servants bustling around in order to change the royal pair for the event. Sherrod and Millie, the couple's man servant and hand maid, led the throng, and in a whirlwind of scrubbing, fabric, and jewels, the couple was deemed ready.

*   *   *

Flanx and Aurastia stood in the throne room of the castle, milling amongst the other nobles. Well, Aurastia was milling, Flanx had been sent on a mission to find what was blocking Zaltreous' ability to scry within the castle walls. Zaltreous had told Aurastia, while sitting by the fire one night, about his trials and tribulations suffered at the hands of the would-be king. He explained how he had escaped, having chipped away at the mortar in the walls with a spoon until he was able to pull the packets free from between the brickwork.

Aurastia, suspecting Aylan's preference for the use of plants, and knowing her talent for herbology, considered the possibility that perhaps there were more packets or potions in place for foiling their attempt to scry.

As a result, Flanx was poking around tapestries, and looking at the brickwork to see if new mortar had been poured. So far he had found nothing.

A fanfare sounded and a pretentious noble with a pointy black beard and dressed in bright yellow and black velvet entered. He clapped his hands loudly and called to all "Places, places everyone!"

The nobility filed to their places at either side of the room, and others took up their positions within the procession. Aurastia found her way to the door, where she would walk behind those bearing the crown and sceptre of the kingdom. The queen mother entered first, looking as regal as ever in her deep red dress lined with gold. Next, Oslan entered with Aylan walking at his left side. Aurastia's mouth fell open in surprise when she saw the other mage. This was not the freckled and unsure child that Zaltreous had boasted of capturing so easily a year ago. This was a woman, pure and simple, and a strong one at that. The set of her jaw and the self-control and beauty she possessed created a pang of jealousy in Aurastia's dark heart.

The nobles carrying the crown and scepter came next, followed by Aurastia who was handed the chalice, then came another rather foul smelling noble carrying the pitcher of wine.

Walking so close behind the royal pair, Aurastia was able to consider the power that the other woman held, and she wondered if Aylan had put any wards against danger upon the prince. Aurastia assumed that she had, after all, Aurastia would have if she were in Aylan's place. There the poor prince walked along, so assured of safety, when not five steps behind him followed a dangerous foe indeed. Aylan, she thought, was much smarter than he, for Aurastia could tell the woman was tense, ready for a fight if a conflict were to arise.

*   *   *

Oslan walked with the procession, fully aware of the danger that followed him. The tiny hairs on the back of his neck bristled at the thought of bearing his back, while empty handed, to the enemy. He had to concentrate hard to keep his hands from balling up into fists, and refused to let his right hand twitch toward the sword-hilt of Skirdkhen, that he wore at his side. He found himself deeply attuned to the jingling of her earrings and necklace that she wore, so close behind him was she. He walked on, all bravery and trust in the woman he loved.

They reached the bottom of the five short steps that would bring them up to the platform that the thrones sat upon. Taking his place in front of the centre throne, the king's throne, he sat and waited for the crown to be placed upon his head by his mother. The queen moved to do so, her body and dress temporarily blocking his view of the nobles with the wine and chalice.

Drat! He thought with a stab of fear, *the one person I need to be wary of, and I've lost sight of her completely.* Suspense and anxiety made his stomach churn. He began to feel ill, and for the first time, started to doubt his own decision of having the dangerous noble here. After all, what had he really succeeded in doing? Had he gained anything from this experience? He had hoped to speak with her, to get an idea of her intentions, or to determine what kind of foe she would prove to be. Was she cunning, or was she all just looks?

Surprisingly, he found that although he knew that she had killed a man, and that she could possibly poison him right here in front of his kingdom, it did not detract from the slight pull he felt from her beauty.

Pain exploded in his foot as Aylan's heel came down hard on his toes.

"Oops, excuse me, Your Grace." She said in an overly sweet voice, taking a moment to bat her long lashes at him innocently. She meant to do that! Now what had she gone and all but crushed his poor foot for? Had he been caught staring? A hot ball of guilt burned heavily in his stomach. He was only trying to get a closer look at the enemy. Well, mostly. What was his wife worried about anyway, clearly the baroness was the enemy, and besides, he was a married man!

And then Aurastia was in front of him, distracting him from his train of thought. His eyes were once again drawn to the sleek lines of her face. All he could think about was his close proximity to possible danger, and it was time to take his drink.

The Queen, having placed the crown upon his head and having addressed the court for their approval, was now moving away. The Baroness drew closer, holding out the chalice filled with a dark red wine that matched the shade of her lips. The prince stared, wondering at its true contents as she proffered him the cup with a single lilting address, "Your Majesty". He took it with only slightly shaking hands, and noticed her swallow perceptively. She seemed to shift nervously, a movement that took away from her gracefulness, and without breaking his gaze from her unfathomable dark brown eyes, he took a long sip from the chalice. He swallowed, feeling Aylan tense at his side, and he finally closed his eyes to feel the effect that the wine would take over him. He felt the cool trickle as the wine made its way down his gullet into the pit of his stomach. The familiar ball of heat formed in his tummy as the wine hit his system, and he felt the heat in his veins. He waited a few seconds more, wondering if he would feel the sting of a poison, his mind attempting to play tricks on him. The temperature seemed to rise and his palms broke out in a sweat. When his father had been poisoned, he had first started to cough. Oslan began to feel a tickle in the back of his throat, and tried to supress the feeling by swallowing hard. Moments ticked past, and he opened his eyes, smiling reassuringly, triumphantly at Aylan. The wine was perfect. His smile didn't falter until he saw the look of confused horror on Aylan's face.

Chapter 31
~ No Effect ~

As Aylan realized he was fine, and replaced the look on her face with an expression of joy, Oslan regained his composure and began to feel the knot in his stomach ease as the rest of the ceremony passed without incident. The scepter was presented to the new king and the nobles accepted their ruler with cheers of acclamation.

Endalwynndale had been a kingdom of peace for generations, and the feeling of relief in the room was palpable now that the realm had a ruler once again. The uncertainty of having no king upon the throne since King Eurilas had been poisoned was over for his subjects, but Oslan's type of rein would be a new one. He still intended to rule as a fair and just king, however, as his forefathers before him had held Skirdkhen as a symbol of peace in the kingdom, he instead wore the famous sword by his side. He had already wielded the weapon in battle against Zaltreous once, and he was prepared to use it again should the necessity arise. His grandfather had been crowned Jonnohlenn the Gentle, and his father had been Eurilas the Stalwart. A great deal of pride and relief swept through him, causing him to close his eyes and swallow slowly while he murmured a quick prayer of thanks to all that was bright, as the first cheer rang out when he was dubbed Oslan the Brave.

After the ceremony, he and Aylan rushed down the corridor, Oslan soaring with so much bliss that he was hard pressed to keep his fast footfalls from skipping or trotting along. Aylan walked swiftly attempting to stay by his side, now a queen in her own right. The severe look on her face was reminiscent of royalty, but even that couldn't dampen his elated mood.

"Oslan, slow down!" She cried in a hushed voice as she fell behind again, "I must talk to you, it's important!"

He bobbed along, the excitement of the day invigorating him and not allowing him to slow. "Aylan, I know what you are going to say, but there was no poison in the wine, I feel fine." He responded while he continued to move. He knew that sometimes marriage came with nagging, any woman who cared for you would do so enough to annoy you at some times, but he wasn't going to let that bother him, not today. She could complain about his carelessness tomorrow.

"It's not about the wine, but that is a good point, we should discuss your wanton disregard for your own safety too!" She retorted strongly. "Will you please wait up? It's hard to walk with this horrendous gown on, and if you plan on insisting that I wear more in the future, then by the shields of the army of Ormond, you will walk at a speed that is manageable for me!."

Oslan loved the dresses she donned, they made her look beautiful and he found himself in awe of her with each new design she wore. He stopped at once to let her catch up, and was immediately knocked forward a few steps as she walked plum into the back of him.

She let out an unladylike, "Oof!" as they collided. He turned quickly to steady her, his athletic instincts taking over. Grasping her arms, he looked earnestly into her eyes and reassured her again, firmly.

"My love, you are the queen now, and I am your king. I have helped to rule this country my whole life, and you need to learn to trust that I know what I am doing. I am aware that you think my choice was one that only a dullard would make, and I know it put me in danger, but sometimes a well-planned strategy can prevent an actual altercation or give us the advantage, saving many lives of the men that would fight for me. I have to think of their families too."

She sighed heavily, but acquiesced. "Very well, I will not bring up the poison again," She allowed, and the sense of triumph washing over him was exquisite, though short lived as she added "today." Inwardly, he groaned. "But there is a bigger issue," she confided, lowering her voice as a troupe of nobles wandered by, gossiping and stopping long enough to bow to the royal couple. She continued when they left, after giving them time to get far enough ahead that they would not overhear. "It is imperative that we get the circlet if we are to have any chance at all of survival in the battle against Zaltreous."

He recognized the need in her voice, and his stomach tightened. "We will attempt to capture it, Darling, I have faith in our lads, we should be able to return with it successfully."

"No, you don't understand Oslan, we *need* it. Zaltreous is powerful enough with the *Almatraek Dím*, but I fear she is more powerful than him."

"What do you mean?" he asked alarm edging into his voice.

"The packets we used to drain Zaltreous' magical ability when he was prisoner, I made one and had the blacksmith hide it within the metal base of the chalice she was to hold. It was strong too. But she carried that thing all throughout the ceremony, and didn't even flinch, let alone swoon at the loss of power."

"But you were standing next to me, and you were fine." He pointed out, alarmed. Perhaps its strength was diminished when it was encased in the metal." He reasoned.

"No, Millie and Thornton went with me to the blacksmith, just in case. I couldn't touch the chalice. When my hand grew close, I found myself tired immediately, and I needed Millie's support to make it back to the castle."

Oslan was struck with a sense of irony as he opened his mouth to chastise her about taking risks that were unnecessary, and changed his mind. He let her speak instead.

"Correct me if I'm wrong, but she seemed absolutely fine to me during the ceremony."

"So were you," he pointed out seriously. "How did you manage that?"

"I cast a ward on myself against that particular spell so I would be free from its effects."

Oslan grew very still, thinking for a few minutes before responding. "Perhaps she had a similar ward? If you were going into a lion's den of your enemies, complete with armed guards and another mage, wouldn't you have prepared yourself much like you did today?"

"I suppose," she said doubtfully, "but how would she know what to protect against? There are no wards that I know of that are all encompassing. You have to ward yourself against each symptom, or ward the route the magic takes to affect you. You can't simply ward against magic, or your own magic would be affected."

"If she wasn't planning on using her magic today," he pondered out loud, "perhaps she did just that."

"That would leave her so defenseless." Aylan remarked, and Oslan could see her slight shutter. "I don't think I would ever take that chance."

"And you will never have to." He told her

protectively. "Come, we must go to the feast. You look stunning, and as king, I intend to promenade you around on the dance floor. The good news is that if she is warded, she will cause us no harm." He could see the resigned disbelief in her eyes, but she turned, looping her arm through his, and he strolled with her to the ballroom at a much slowed pace. Although he had begun to look forward to the evening's celebration, Oslan would now have this tugging at the back of his mind. Perhaps he should offer the baroness a dance. This would afford him the opportunity to question her under the cover of the music. However, even if she was warded, it would be a dangerous move. All it would take would be a well-placed dagger on the noble's part and everything would end.

Chapter 32
~ Don't Scry Over Spilt Milk ~

Flanx anxiously hid himself amongst the servers and other workers of the castle. True, his white garb was unlike the castle livery's grey-brown and black colours, but with his downcast eyes and his humble stance, any noble would know him for a servant nonetheless. He moved through the kitchen and swiped one of the many metal pitchers of wine standing on a table. He kept walking, intent showing on his aged face. Trying to hide the trepidation he felt, he carried the vessel to the double doors that led to the throne room and ambled past the guards into the feast.

Amazingly, the room had been transformed. Tables stood up and down the hall where nobles had gathered during the ceremony, and minstrels played from a platform to the side of the dais that held the thrones and head table. Later, there would be dancing, but for now, the air was filled with the hearty smells of meat, bread, and steaming root vegetables. People began to enjoy the repast by spearing pieces of food on the tips of their knives and popping the morsels into their mouths. Flanx shuttered inwardly as meat juice ran through the smacking lips of a tubby man engaged in conversation while he ate. He watched in disgust as it dripped down over the man's chin onto his tunic while he talked, and a large piece of semi-chewed meat showed in his mouth as he pronounced his vowels. Ironically, Flanx's tummy grumbled, reminding him that it had been some hours since his last meal, but he knew he would not partake of the succulent delicacies he traversed. He tore his eyes away from the spectacle of the fat man's meal, and thought that was probably best anyway.

The celebrations gave Flanx a chance to blend in and walk around the room's perimeter with his jug. When a noble called to him for more wine, he obliged, but for the most part, he was left unbothered. It was his careful skirting of the room and tripping by chance that allowed him to find the first of Aylan's protective packets. As a guest stumbled past him to the water-closet, and rudely pushed him back against the wall, the heel of Flanx's boot caught the edge of a tapestry that hung to the floor. After a brief moment of terror while Flanx juggled the bumped jug so as not to spill the staining wine on himself or the noble, he felt the hard lump under him, and saw that the tapestry was not flush against the stone wall. Shifting it slightly with his toe and exposing a small bulge, he quickly knelt with hope in his throat, and pulled the tapestry back further to reveal the plain tied packet of herbs. Leaving it there, he deftly tipped his wine pitcher, and poured some of the dark red liquid onto the packet. Instantly, the packet seemed to shrivel slightly, as if some of its contents had been dissolved by the wine.

Excitement bubbled up inside him. *A triumph!* He thought proudly. He stood, replaced the tapestry over the ruined packet, and now knowing what he was looking for, continued to skirt the room for more.

*   *   *

Back in the narrow laboratory in Entwhilen, Zaltreous had finished his meal, and turned the pages of one of Aurastia's spell books with slightly greasy fingers. Making an effort not to leave stains on the rather old looking pages, he bellowed for a servant again.

In her absence, he had taken the time to sort through her older spell books, and had begun copying some of the nastier spells into the blank pages at the end of the *Almatraek Dim*. As with the other spells in the book, the mage that entered them had to add four drops of his or her own blood to the ink used, to bind the spells with magical energy. He now wore a cloth wrapped around his right palm as a bandage, to cover the spot he had poked with his dagger to take the blood. He heard the servant approaching noisily down the hall, grumbling loudly as he came. Zaltreous took a break from reading and copying, to blow on the ink to make it dry before closing the *Almatraek Dim.*

He decided to try scrying on the castle in Endalwynndale once more. His eyes scanned the surface of the water in the bowl, and he froze, his breath hitching in his throat in pleasant surprise. The reflection of the ceiling of thin room swirled away and the throne room in Endalwynndale became visible, then faded, and solidified again. Zaltreous shot up in elation, shocking the servant that had entered. The man jumped back, and his elbow caught Zaltreous' glass of milk, sending it spilling across the table. The thick white liquid flew into the bowl, and a splash landed across the pages of Aurastia's ancient book.

Horrified, Zaltreous watched the scene unfold in what seemed like slow motion. With his concentration gone, the throne room disappeared in the bowl, and the milk seeped into the page of writing, marring the ink. Zaltreous watched, dumbfounded, as the black-red ink bled across the parchment, ruining the spell. With a primal cry of fury, Zaltreous channeled his energy and incanted a quick levitation spell, hurling it at the other man. The servant, apologising profusely, was lifted off his feet, and was thrown toward the open window and out. There was a dull thud as he hit the courtyard below. Zaltreous stood looking at the window, stunned. He had acted in rage, and it was the first time that he had successfully used his magic to kill. His first thought was *What have I done?* But as his initial panic subsided, he reconsidered, a darkness falling into his heart. Then the only evil thought that remained was: *Now that wasn't so hard after all.*

Chapter 33
~ Rope Trick ~

It took weeks for Oslan and his party of companions to sail across the Ocean of Empathy to the dark forest of Evenwood, where the Cyclops, Augle, was reported to live. In the belly of the boat, so far from home, Oslan thought wistfully of the sound of their families bidding them farewell at the docks with the common wish of good tidings: "May brightness be behind you." He hoped it would be. He always felt anxious when he was away from his kingdom, although he knew it was in the capable hands of the queen mother, and his three sisters. He donned his thick black leather glove, and took up the jesses of his falcon, Archer. Beside him, Aylan did the same for Swiftwing. This would be the first time she had taken her saker away from the kingdom, and he knew she was nervous about him getting lost. He gave her a reassuring smile, and stepped closer. With his free hand, he tenderly tucked a stray piece of hair behind her ear. "I love you," he reminded her.

"And I you," she replied. He let his lips briefly brush against hers and withdrew. It was his tradition to steal a kiss for luck before any contest, and this day could very well end in battle.

"Shall we?" he asked, and allowed her to climb the steps to the deck above them, while still relishing the feel of her soft kiss. Even when she dressed in a tunic for battle, he thought she was the most beautiful creature in the world.

They prepared to disembark onto the tiny rowboat that would take them to the edge of the land proper, and Oslan conceded that perhaps it was a good thing that Aylan had convinced Sasha to wear a tunic as well, instead of the ornate gowns she usually favoured. His wife had already shimmied down the rope to the awaiting craft floating on the uneven waves that would row them ashore. But now Sasha, clinging to the wet cord, seemed to be stuck as she dangled half way down to the rowboat. Every time a wave rolled, moving the ship and rope in her hands, she squealed in a decidedly unladylike manner, and hugged the knotted line tighter. They all went about encouraging her down in different ways.

"Why did we have to drop anchor here?" She wined in a decidedly un-Sasha-like tone. "Because," Carn informed her from his place in the rowboat, "There are no docks here, and we have to keep the ship safe. If we sailed any closer to the shore, she'd become grounded when the tide went out."

Sasha gulped and shut her eyes to the moving boats beside and under her, still not budging an inch.

Never one to have a lot of patience, Oslan merely tried to order her down. To his dismay, it didn't work. Carn offered to climb back up to fetch her, but as his weight made the rope move under her, her terrified yelp made him stop. Aylan tried coaxing her down with friendly words of advice, and that seemed to bring her out of her shell a little. Long enough, at least, for her to raise her head, open her eyes, and look down, at which point she began to look decidedly green. In the end, it had been the threat of fame that did it.

After waiting for what seemed like an eternity, Thorn finally called up to her. "This is how it is. I'm finding this whole thing rather amusing. How do you think the people at court will laugh at the tale when I sing them the song I am composing at this moment about a beauty stuck in the air."

"You wouldn't!" She admonished vehemently from where she dangled.

"The way I see it, I have till you reach the boat," was his eager reply. He cleared his throat, and in a strong, ringing voice began to sing:

> "Sasha, the maiden bright,
> Held onto the rope so tight,
> The waves did turn,
> The sea she spurned,
> And her head became quite light."

With this, Sasha seemed to collect herself inwardly. She tentatively lowered herself another foot. Trembleton elbowed Thorn and crowed, "It's working, keep singing!"

A broad grin spread across Thorn's face and he continued:

> "Her face started to look green,
> 'Twas the funniest thing I'd seen,
> She clung to the rope,
> Without a hope,
> Of looking where she'd been."

Fraught with anger, Sasha seemed to forget her fear, and shakily began to climb down at a good clip. But, Thorn was merciless and continued till her slippered toes actually touched the seat of the boat.

> "For the rest of us, quite a thrill,
> But for her, a reason to kill,
> She's no longer stuck,
> And now I must duck,
> Or out 'o the boat we'll spill."

The boys began to hoot and holler as Carn offered Sasha his steady arm, which she took gratefully while shooting Thorn a black look indeed. She consoled herself with taking a seat next to Aylan, where she knew she would receive some sympathy. The rest of the group joined them in the boat, and Carn began to row them ashore.

They were an impressive sight indeed, with their silvery armour brightly reflecting the sun like the waves around them. The symbol of the dragon's head blowing fire adorned each of their chests, and the wind billowed the capes that some of them wore.

There had been a harrowing moment back in the palace as they were collecting their things, when Oslan had to call his mage to the armoury to ask her how to take down his beautiful fire-blasting shield without killing himself. She explained that it was perfectly safe to touch. It required the force of a blow from an arrow or weapon to discharge. Although she did half-jokingly warn him not to get kicked by a horse while he carried it, lest he end up with a roasted steed.

The shield sat proudly in front of him now, flower shining as brightly as his kingdom's insignia. Archer and Swiftwing perched comfortably on the royal couple's gloves, and seemed to enjoy the feel of the salt air ruffling their feathers. Oslan was happy to have them along, their food was becoming scarce, but if the birds did their job right, the group would be having meat with their suppers again. The king was confident that they would be, but he wondered what else they would encounter in the looming, dark forest laid out before them.

Chapter 34
~ Seeing Eyes to Eye ~

Before long, the knight's continuous rowing brought them to a space in the forest edge where they could disembark and pull their rowboat up onto the land to await their return trip. Oslan was surprised at the feel of the forest as they began to edge closer to the first few trees that grew there. He had expected that as they drew nearer to the shore, the forest would seem to lighten as their eyes adjusted to the evening light. He thought they would have hours yet to walk before they would need to make camp for the night. But now he stared uneasily at the thick rough bark that looked almost black. He noticed that the branches seemed to jut out at awkward angles, like they were preparing to reach for his party, making the trees seem even more sinister.

Outwardly, he showed no fear, but inwardly, his skin crawled.

"I don't like the looks of this." Trembleton complained matter-of-factly. Oslan silently agreed with him. Sometimes it was a chore to be brave. But brave he would be. "We will stay together, and keep an eye out in all directions. We will be fine," he reassured his band.

Archer adjusted his weight on Oslan's arm, reminding the king that he was still there. "We'll send them out to fetch our supper," he said to Aylan while motioning to his bird. "We will feel better about this when we have full bellies." He caught the uneasy look on her face and elected to free his falcon first, so she would be put at ease. "They won't get lost, Aylan, Swiftwing will always find you." He reassured her. He released Archer and nodded to his wife. With a sigh, she also sent her fowl into the sky to see what they could find.

Oslan watched in satisfaction as she lowered her arm, and her cloak closed protectively in front of her. The beautifully ornate embroidered stars stood out brightly along the trim of the navy blue cloak. The only drawback to bringing the birds was that as long as she allowed Swiftwing to perch on her arm, her cloak would remain open, leaving her vulnerable. He couldn't have that. Now that it was covering her though, he felt a wave of anxiety lift.

He motioned for the others to form up, taking positions around the women. He and Carn led, followed by Aylan and Sasha, and then Bowregard, Thorn and Trembleton took up the rear of the expedition. As they were discussing how to cut a path through the forest, Sasha called out for them to wait. "There are things ahead, evil things that will be alerted to our presence. There is something inherently wrong with them...they wish us harm without being provoked. And there is something else..." her voice trailed off as Oslan felt goose-bumps rise on his arms at her words. She continued, "I see deformations, like the Cyclops only having one eye. They move strangely. I don't like this at all!" she seconded Trembleton's earlier announcement.

Oslan found the moon that was beginning to rise, and was relieved to see that it was full, giving off lots of light. However, glancing again into the forest, he observed that the moonbeams were strangely unable to penetrate the thick boughs of the trees, leaving their way almost completely dark.

"Perhaps we should wait till the light of morning," Thorn suggested, "I don't know about making camp here, perhaps we should row back to the ship-"

"No need for that," Sasha interrupted, "This

will be fine." And with that she stubbornly plunked down on a fallen tree trunk and crossed her arms so as not to be argued with.

"The ship would really be the safest place to spend the night." Bowregard said matter-of-factly, but Sasha gave him such a hard stare that he finished with: "But this looks perfectly acceptable too."

The king sighed inwardly, and for just a split second, entertained the thought of asking Aylan to put some kind of sleep spell on Sasha so they could carry her quickly and quietly back up the rope. The earful they'd get in the morning wouldn't be worth it though, and the spell might cloud her seeing skills. Best to just set up a watch and keep guard all night in case something came for them out of the forest.

The night passed uneventfully for the most part, except for the critters the birds managed to bring back for their meal. One was a small rodent that looked sickly, and only had three legs. On its head, where its eyes should have been, there was just fur like the stuff that covered the rest of its face. It had an oversized nose to make up for the lost sense, and it wriggled feebly in Swiftwing's unyielding grasp. Archer fared slightly better, returning with a bird that looked normal. Perhaps, it had migrated and flown into this evil-looking place, and so wasn't under the effect of whatever had inflicted the other animals that lived here. They chose to eat the bird, but only Trembleton was willing to sample the rat thing. He took first watch, as he ended up retching through half the night.

In the morning, the king was relieved to see that though only dimly, the branches were letting through some of the early morning light. Although strangely, the sound of birdcalls that should have flooded the forest remained uncannily absent.

They broke camp and set off at a quick pace between the trees, not wanting to spend a night still in the woods if it wasn't strictly necessary. There was no clear-cut path, so the band had to forge one as they walked. They moved carefully, trying not to step on the scraggly vegetation whenever a clear foot fall was visible. The branches clawed at the men's armour and created a chilling sound like long nails running across a piece of slate, which made the hair at the back of their necks stand on end.

At one point the king's foot came down on a kind of beetle with a sickening crunch. When Oslan lifted his foot to remark what he had stepped on, his tummy lurched at the sight of what was left oozing there. He wiped his foot off on a nearby tree trunk, and he began being more cautious about where he placed his feet. Partway through the day, Carn stopped the party and quickly knelt on the path they were creating. He had found a dark string, like a pull-rope, and followed it to what looked like a small box trap. It was shoddy looking, as if it had been made by a child, although Carn had to admit that it looked like it just might work.

"Heads up lads, this could get interesting." He announced in a low voice, "We have signs of intelligent life. This could be what we're looking for."

They proceeded, and each one took care to take high steps over the wire so as not to spring the trap.

Oslan heard Sasha remarking to Aylan quietly about the ease of movement the tunics afforded them, and that she should have abandoned her gowns long ago if this was the trade-off. The king shook his head, and wondered if this adventure would spawn a new trend in his kingdom. He hoped not, he rather preferred the dresses, and it had taken so much work initially to get his wife to wear one. Although, truth be told, the hose she wore with her tunics did much to flatter her long legs which would otherwise be obscured by any gown. Sighing, he continued on, and resigned himself to the knowledge that only time would unfold what was to be. Although, he supposed that if worse came to worse and Sasha did decide to take up the habit of wearing men's clothes, he could always hire Thorn to sing her back into a gown.

It was not long after that when Sasha swooned, and told them to release the birds. She refused to say more, except that it was after noon, and they should consider a repast. Oslan couldn't help but notice a guilty look cross her face, but he and Aylan did as she instructed, hoping fervently that Archer and Swiftwing would return with more birds from outside of the forest instead of creatures from within.

It was then that they discovered that wood from the forest wouldn't burn. The vegetation was covered in what seemed like tiny hairs, and each hair was covered in a thin layer of mucus. Eventually, Aylan ended up simply conjuring a fire, but it wasn't to burn long. For Archer returned then, empty handed, and without the other Falcon. Aylan was distraught, and couldn't hold her concentration on her spell. Her energy left the fire, and the flames died. Oslan tried to console her, and questioned Sasha as to the whereabouts of the bird. She was also upset, and confided that the bird was still safe for now, but that they had to move quickly to keep it that way.

They released Archer once more, following the direction he took off in, and soon came upon a hollow in a hill. Upon closer inspection, they recognized that it was the entranceway to a cave.

Black stones were set into the hillside, sunken deep into the earth. The boulders looked almost as if the ground was trying to swallow them, and they appeared to be wet, though there was no water source to be seen.

Oslan heard the others draw their weapons, and motioned for them to continue on silently, when Archer cried out and Swiftwing's terrified *Ki-yee* came as a response from within the bowels of the cave.

Lumbering footfalls that shook the forest came next, and in the following moments, a hulking figure of a man all but filled the entranceway to the cave. He was armed with a gnarled knotted club in one hand, and held Swiftwing upside down like a stewing chicken in the other.

"Swiftwing!" Aylan cried out in distress, then almost unintelligibly, she hissed "Fuer!" *Fire!* Oslan felt the burst of heat as a fireball popped into existence above her hand to his left.

He cursed under his breath. Feeling like he was about to lose control of the situation, he tried to rein her flare of emotion in. "Blast it Aylan, hold!" he urged too low for anyone else to hear. "You would not want to risk cooking Swiftwing like a goose, think now!"

"Do you really think my aim so bad? This is what I intend to do if he hurts my falcon," was her pointed response. "One shot, right between the...er, *in* the eye?" She finished in an almost confused voice.

No one else moved, for they were all mesmerized by the sight of the giant's wisps of sparse hair, his gnashing mouth, and his solitary angry eye.

Chapter 35
~ Moonstruck ~

Within her fortress walls, Aurastia's anger flared. "I leave you alone for one week, and come home to find that mess out there on the cobblestones?"

"Come now Aurastia, I had the servants take care of that."

"The body yes, but what about the *stair*? If you're going to play at being evil Zaltreous, you must learn to properly clean up after yourself, or you will get us all caught. I am a baroness, not a captain, and I do not intend to go down with the flaming ship!"

Zaltreous had never seen the other mage lose her cool enough to curse. It was almost enough to make him stop and think about what wanted to fly from his mouth, but emotions were running high for everyone in the room.

"I am not *playing* at being evil," he spat the offending word, "I only want what should rightfully be mine!"

"What should rightfully be yours?" Aurastia questioned, "And what's that? Revenge, the king's life, the castle? You had a crush on a girl and she turned you down. Nobody owes you anything. You are no more than a child who has lost its plaything."

"A child... who has lost its plaything." Zaltreous repeated the words, tasted them, let them roll of his tongue in a voice no higher than a whisper. He contemplated the room; the six guards standing at the ready, her two servants on either side of the door, Flanx unobtrusively stoking the fireplace and she in the middle of the floor. He said "Fli," *Levitate,* and lifted a finger, just one. All ten people in the room rose off the floor. He bound them all with magic, leaving them helpless to move, and approached her.

"Tay ka Ey tari traek sauxlija. Vear Ey, Aurastia, kyl ka Tay jaro Ey postik joiyat pineom Tay ot pos Ey? Xa fitiyat eyt tririt ot ine Tay jaro Ey joiyat postoiyat nal Tayt kala." *You do me a great injustice. Tell me, Aurastia, why do you think I have been allowing you to rule me? It suited my purpose to let you think I was possessed by your beauty.*

"Ey jaxa alayn Tay roga so talai!" *I can help you take the castle!* she implored.

He laughed. "Ey jar ha rogaom box se so talai. In tan, Ey rauxliya fallot jus Ey postai taritae nula Endalwynndale, est Ey gellusliya umek Tay." *I plan on taking more than the castle. In fact, I will not stop until I control all of Endalwynndale, and I will start with you.* He closed in on her, and grabbed her by the hair at the back of her head.

Helpless to move, and neck muscles tensed uncomfortably in the position he held her in, she purred gently: "Tay karaux dir ot rohegah Ey, Ey jo falima tayt." *You do not need to conquer me, I am already yours.*

"Ey xaro." *I know.* He smiled a cold dangerous smile before he backed away from her and released her hair. Freeing the two servants by the door, he switched back to the common tongue to bark commands. "You there, you heard your mistress, there is a mess outside in need of some attention. Clean it up!"

The servants ran from the room to attend to the chore without even glancing at Aurastia for the signal to go ahead with the order. *Very good,* Zaltreous congratulated himself, *now we're finally getting somewhere.* "We will leave on the morrow for Endalwynndale," he informed them as he released his spells on them one by one. He left

Flanx for last, purely out of spite for the old man. He waited to see if any of the guards would attack or if the other mage would argue, but each person in the room just stood there as if waiting to hear his edict. *Very good indeed.*

"Flanx did a good job while you were serving the king, I have been scrying the castle over the days it took you to return home. It is the perfect time to strike. Oslan and his new queen have left it in search of the circlet, so it is ours for the taking."

"But why?" she asked in a trembling voice quite unlike her usual purr. "Why not just stay here with me? Aren't you happy here?"

This time he threw back his head when he laughed. "Happy?" he repeated, "Happiness is power. You mocked me for being sore over a girl. That might have been the case in the beginning, but my ambitions have grown tenfold since then. Why would I settle for a palace when I could have the entire kingdom?"

"But," she protested, "my fortress-"

Zaltreous closed his eyes and pulled forth a torrent of vitality from his core. Hitting all present with an umbrella like shield, he unleashed a blast of energy that poured through the floor. All was momentarily silent as the magic seeped through the floorboards. Then, as suddenly as his initial onslaught, the torrent travelled up the walls and into the ceiling. All of the cracks in the mortar momentarily glowed red, seeming to throb as it gained more of Zaltreous' energy.

The air thickened, and the candles blew out as the temperature in the room swiftly rose. A bead of sweat rolled down the side of the mage's face with his exertion. He could feel his energy draining swiftly, and knew that he would have to end the multiple spells soon, or be left helpless forever. He cast yet another spell, ensnaring the energy of those around him.

He grew stronger as Aurastia, Flanx and the guards weakened. The armour of one of the warriors clanged dully as the man crumpled to the ground, lifeless. Zaltreous didn't care, he poured their energy into his masterpiece. The reddened cracks grew brighter and brighter, some of the stone becoming molten and beginning to drip down the walls. Then, in a final coup, every seam in the building burst apart in an explosion of dust and flying rocks.

Zaltreous was left panting with a grim look on his pale face. He elbowed the sweat from his brow and took a shaky breath, checking to see that he could still feel some energy at his core. It was deeply depleted, but enough lasted.

He allowed the shield to wink out before he strode through the rubble to retrieve the unharmed book. Locating it, he opened a hand toward the tome, catching it when it flew to his hand. He regarded the beautiful mage that stood in shock in the pile of stone that used to be her palace.

"Your palace is no longer an issue." He informed her. "I've changed my mind, I leave today and I will strike under the light of the moon. Come with me, or stay here and rebuild, the choice is yours." With that, he left her behind to find a servant to ready the carriage.

Flanx dropped the poker he had been using to stoke the fire before Zaltreous decimated the hall. He hobbled to Aurastia's side. "He appears to have been fooling us with parlour tricks. Fear not, my lady, he may be more than he seems, but you will put him in his place."

She nodded, a distant look in her eyes as if she only half heard him through a dream. Flanx tried again, "We should go to Endalwynndale and let him take over the palace. He just may be able to do it. Let him conquer the kingdom, then we only have to contend with him. While he's busy taking down the guards, I'm sure we could find a spell in the book to aid our cause. Why should the world be his, when it could be yours?"

As he talked, he saw her square her shoulders. She tossed her hair in the confident way she was used to, and he saw the fire return to her eyes. As she moved to follow Zaltreous, Flanx noted that she once again held her head high.

Chapter 36
~ Simple Logic ~

Oslan knew he had to proceed cautiously. Despite the grotesque appearance of this being, he had to keep his eyes on the prize. They were here for the circlet, and there was no need for this encounter to come to blows and more death if they could resolve matters peacefully. With his heart pounding and blood racing in fear, he stepped forward toward the Cyclops and sheathed his sword, hoping that the beast would drop his club. No such luck.

"Augle, I presume?" He said jovially in a clear voice that carried across the clearing.

Augle grunted, but whether in agreement or in response to sound in general, Oslan didn't know. Never having met a Cyclops before, he really wasn't sure how intelligent they were.

"We have come to discuss with you the circlet you hold within, and well, that falcon in your hand."

Augle slowly looked down with furrowed brow, to Swiftwing, then back to the king. When he had fixed Oslan once again in his stare, the gigantic man replied in a deep rumbling slow voice, "bird lunch."

Oslan felt a moment of hopelessness. How would he be able to convince this creature to give them the circlet, let alone free the fowl? From the looks of the trap in the woods, it wouldn't be very effective unless the other critters here were even duller than Augle. The Cyclops must be hungering something fierce, but Oslan was determined, he had found the perfect wedding present for his wife, and he would do everything he could to retrieve the falcon for her.

Oslan felt a momentary stab of fright when suddenly to his right he caught a flash of movement out of the corner of his eye. He looked, his hand going reflexively for his hilt, but there was nobody there save for the other members of his party. It had been only Bowregard, who seemed to randomly loose an arrow almost straight up. Seconds later, a misshapen bird fell into the clearing in front of them, Bow's arrow protruding from its feathery chest.

He calmly picked it up, and Oslan burst with pride at his archer's quick thinking and skill. Bowregard, with a will of steel, advanced toward Augle, holding the bird between them.

"I will trade you your bird for mine, Augle, and then we will both have what we want."

Augle again looked down at his bird, then at the thing skewered on the arrow. "My bird pretty," was his reply.

"Yes Augle, it is our bird. The pretty falcon belongs to the pretty lady. She would like her bird back, but you will not miss your lunch." He motioned with the scrawny bird toward Augle, encouraging him to come get it. Augle looked toward Oslan's left, where he knew the women were standing, and the one-eyed man spoke:

"You share pretty bird lunch?"

To the king's surprise, it was Sasha's voice that answered back. "My bird is not for eating, it is my companion, my friend."

Oslan opened his mouth to correct the Cyclops, and heard his seer clear her voice. He turned his helmet laden head toward her and saw to his surprise, that Aylan was missing. Panic struck then, and it took all his willpower not to draw his sword in response and start a commotion. He tightened his grip on his shield instead and remained silent. He looked around the clearing, but it was as if his wife had disappeared into thin air.

Sasha was mouthing something to him, but he couldn't make it out. Then, he heard a twig snap to the side of the entranceway to the cave, and he understood. When everyone's attention had followed Bowregard's shot, she must have eaten one of her invisibility pills. She was going for the circlet while the Cyclops was distracted. He could have kissed her then, but she had just given her position away. The Cyclops began to turn his head toward the sound, and time seemed to speed up.

Bowregard loosed another arrow, this one passing right by where the twig had snapped. Oslan felt a blanket of cold fear pass through him and his heart leapt into his throat. He knew that Bowregard was trying to cover for his mage, but he knew also that the bowman could not see where she stood. His arrow thudded into the side of a tree, pinning a dying squirrel-thing to its trunk. Bow walked to retrieve it, stepping slightly around a spot on the ground where some leaves seemed to be flattened by an invisible force. *That was close!* Oslan thought. But now they had two things for Augle to eat that they could trade for Swiftwing, and his wife was for the moment in the clear.

*   *   *

Aylan's heart thundered in her chest as Bow's arrow headed toward her face. She squeezed her eyes shut against the anticipated pain and waited breathlessly for the oncoming arrow's impact. She felt her hair lift off the right side of her neck as the arrow flew past, then heard the hollow *thunk* as it speared the tree behind her. Bow walked toward her to retrieve his arrow, and she noticed the lines of sweat that had trickled down the sides of his face. As he walked past, she silently laid a hand on his shoulder to let him know that she was fine. She heard him release his breath, and realized that he had taken a gamble with her life. She couldn't fault him on that though, she was about to do the same thing herself.

As the archer continued to distract the Cyclops, she made her move. She stopped just outside the entrance of the cave and swallowed hard. She didn't know what Augle was doing behind her, or if he had yet noticed her, but she couldn't spare the time to look. She had to have faith in Oslan and their knights. She noticed the floor seemed to change where the stone walls met the forest floor. The soft dirt ground gave way to hard damp stone, and she could see dried white bones littering the area inside. Beyond the bones, the cave darkened, making it harder to see what else may lay there in waiting.

Curious, she chose a leaf that had fallen from a nearby tree out of Augle's line of sight. She whispered "Fli," *Levitate,* so quietly that it rang like silence even to her own ears. The leaf slowly rose into the air and as she moved her hand, it followed, until it hovered a foot above the ground beside her. She sent the leaf flying into the cave. Well, she tried. Upon moving over the spot where the ground changed and the first stone walls grew upward, the leaf stopped in mid-air. Aylan felt her magical energy snap back into her as if it had been slashed with a knife. The leaf see-sawed lazily down to the ground below it as understanding dawned on her as to why she couldn't just levitate the circlet and summon it to her that way.

She wondered if entering the cave would stop the effects of her invisibility pill. She now spared a quick glance back, not at Augle, but at Oslan, whom she feared she might never see again. If she stepped into the cave and became visible, there was no way she could make it back to her friends without Augle noticing that she had tried to trick him. She glanced uneasily at his heavy club. It was very nearly the size of a thick tree branch, and in fact, Aylan was pretty sure that it had been just that before it had become his weapon of choice.

They were all counting on her, and she would do what she could. She knew she didn't have long before they would run out of distractions for the Cyclops. She had to move. She held her hands up and stared at the spot where her palms should be as she walked over the threshold. She felt no different, and saw that her hands remained invisible. With a feeling of relief, she pressed on. As she proceeded into the darker part of the cave, she noticed that the bones of Augle's past meals were growing larger and larger. Her vision was beginning to fail with each step further into the darkness. Her foot bumped something large, and it scuttled away into the dark. Bile rose in her throat. Her skin crawled at the sound and she stifled a scream, not wanting to bring on the rampaging one-eyed giant. She still had a job to do, and she would try to live through it if she could.

She picked her way carefully through the darkness until eventually she noticed a new brightness ahead. She picked her way toward it. It was a pure white light, a shaft of brilliance entering a hole in the cave from above. The sun shone down like a spotlight onto the circlet that sat waiting upon a hewn off stalagmite. She rushed forward then, reaching out her hand to claim it, and stopped when she saw the bony fingers that gipped it from behind.

She wandered around to the far side of the

jutting rock, where she found a skeleton dressed in a long dusty robe. The sleeve had slipped down the arm that had reached for the enchanted crown, and the fingers still remained gripping the fine metal. Its skull however, was crushed on one side. Aylan gulped and listened into the darkness for Augle's return. She heard nothing save for a constant sound of dripping water from some unseen underground stream.

She went for the circlet again. Her hand passed into the sunlight that surrounded it, and she waited with the expectation that something might happen. Nothing did. Her fingers drew nearer to the crafted metal, and everything the imp had told them about it circled in her memory. She hesitated, her fingertips only a centimetre from the beautifully formed crown. She withdrew her hand and pulled her sleeve down over her palm. There was no point in taking chances. Once her fingertips were completely shrouded by the sleeve, she again reached for the circlet.

She wrapped her fingers slowly around it, not knowing what to expect.

Before trying to remove it, she looked at her surroundings nervously for any visible traps that might injure her when she took the crown. She saw nothing obvious that might cause her harm, but magic could be invisible. She grasped the metal and pulled, but to her surprise, it did not budge. She tugged again at the crown, this time bracing her leg against the stalagmite for leverage, and realized that the hand of the skeleton was holding it fast. With a shudder, she used her free hand to begin prying the digits frozen in their death grip, from the fine metal. *If I get out of this alive,* she thought, *Oslan is going to owe me big-time!* The crown came away with a snapping sound, the bones crumbling to dust under the force of her fingers.

With the circlet suddenly released, she fell backwards onto her rump, still holding the crown in her covered hand. She waited again for Augle to come, but the dust settled with only her shaky breathing and the drip of some hidden spring for company. She stowed the very visible circlet in her satchel, and watched it disappear as the invisible cloth shrouded it. She retreated back through the darkness of the cave, hoping she would make it out before the effects of the pill wore off. She could tell the light was growing brighter ahead, and saw Augle still standing with his back to her way out. Careful not to step on any more twigs that might snap under her weight, she emerged into the forest once more.

*   *   *

"Augle, have you ever seen a bird like this?" Oslan asked while motioning at the incensed Swiftwing still dangling from his meaty fist.

Augle looked at the falcon, with its perfect gimlet eyes and sleek form. "Pretty bird," was Augle's reply.

Oslan nodded, knowingly. "That's right Augle, he came here with us and is not from this forest," he explained as if to a child. "If you ate him, you would likely become very ill, as our companion did when he ate a fowl that you are used to eating from the Evenwood Forest."

Augle lifted Swiftwing roughly to look at him, his brow furrowed over his one huge eye, a look of confusion on his gigantic face. Swiftwing flapped his wings and let out another unappreciative "*Ki-yee*".

The king continued, "We will trade you these *two* beasts for your lunch, if you will return my lady's pet."

Augle's brow furrow deepened for a split second, and then his countenance brightened. "Two *more* than one!" He announced proudly. "Agreed, I give you one, you give me two! He, he! Augle smarter than fancy man!" Then once more his countenance fell. "That Augle's outside the head voice."

"That's alright Augle," replied the king, "I'll still trade you." Augle brightened again.

"Fancy man nice," he said, now contrite. They made the switch, and Augle crowed loudly with delight. He turned to go back to his cave, and Oslan's heart leapt up into his throat. *What if Aylan is still in there, she'll be trapped!* His mind raced frantically, trying to come up with a way to lure Augle back out into the open again. He felt the pressure of fingertips on his side where there was a space in his armour. He nearly jumped out of his skin at the unexpected pressure, and the sound of Aylan's sweet voice shushing him. She was back then, and they could leave. They should beat a hasty retreat back to their ship; they may only have moments before Augle noticed that the circlet was gone.

Chapter 37
~ A Sight for Sore Eyes ~

Filled with the trepidation of pursuit, Oslan, the women, and his knights hurried back to their row boat without incident. *Augle must be enjoying his lunch and must not yet have noticed the circlet missing,* Oslan figured. He felt more relieved once he had climbed the dangling rope and was finally able to set foot on the ship's deck. He was glad that the Cyclops was for the moment content, he seemed like a simple and misunderstood beast.

Oslan turned and proffered his hand, ready to help one of the ladies up into the boat, when without warning Aylan began to speak in Almatrae. With a mischievous expression on her face as she faced his seer, his wife raised her hand, causing Sasha to levitate straight up into the air. Aylan's spell dropped the other woman onto the deck, and to her credit, Sasha almost kept her footing. She let out a brief humiliated shriek as she plopped down onto her rump after pin-wheeling arms couldn't save her. Oslan helped her up while trying to suppress a grin. Aylan shimmied up the rope and offered the all-too-innocent explanation that she had simply tried to avoid Sasha's problem with the rope completely.

They dropped the sails and headed post haste back to Endalwynndale. The Ocean of Empathy was eerily calm on the return trip, as if waiting for a massive storm to hit. Oslan didn't like it, it put him on edge, and his previous feeling of unease returned. With no breeze, the ship barely moved, and he had to get Aylan to conjure some wind so they could make good time.

The sense of electricity in the air as they got closer to his kingdom was palpable. Oslan could feel all the hair on his arms lift, and felt an undeniable tingle at the base of his neck. He saw Aylan absently rubbing the vine tattoo from their wedding day, and realized that his was tingling under his skin. Upon coming into viewing distance of their home, Thorn called down in alarm from the crow's nest: "Nobody's moving, Highnesses. Everything is as still as the water." His spyglass scanned the kingdom laid out before them as he talked. Something was amiss. Normally on an afternoon like this, peasants would be working in the fields, nobles would be shopping in the marketplace, and the din of the workers on the docks should be heard by them already. Instead, they were greeted with silence.

Thorn climbed down the rigging to the deck, and bade Oslan look through his telescopic lens. Oslan did, and was struck dumb by what he saw. All across his vantage point, the people of his kingdom appeared to be frozen in mid activity. People who had been shopping at stalls were paralyzed in various poses; paying for wares, reaching out to inspect goods, walking in pairs, even a boy and dog with joyous expressions on their faces frozen mid-flight through a game of chase.

"Aylan, what manner of magic is this?" Oslan questioned his mage as he handed her the spyglass. "Did you have no visions of this abomination?" He asked Sasha, who simply shook her head in awe as unmoving people began to be visible to the naked eye.

"I knew that Swiftwing would lead us to the Cyclops," she said guiltily as Aylan shot her a look of hurt and surprise, "but I had no hint of this in my visions," she finished confidently.

Aylan's brow furrowed, and Oslan knew that meant she was trying to puzzle it out. "It was one big spell, nobody went walking through the town hitting people with it," she said quietly as she thought it through. "You can tell by the expression on their faces. No one is surprised or afraid, you only see the regular emotions you would expect. This happened to them all at once."

"Now the question is," pondered the king aloud as their boat reached the dock, "why are we not being affected by the spell?"

"The magic must have only affected the people present at the time it was cast, although, I marvel at the size of the blast radius of the spell," Aylan answered. "I haven't seen anything like this before, it is as if the whole market is affected, perhaps the whole kingdom."

"Are they even alive?" Bowregard wondered aloud, "Can they see, hear, or feel anything?"

Aylan just shook her head in bewilderment, and then answered. "I do not know, I have never heard of the likes of a spell quite like this."

"We must get to the castle quickly to see the full extent of the harm done." Oslan reasoned. "I need to make sure my mother and sisters are alright."

"I would like to get us to my workroom," Aylan added, "hopefully it remains a secret, and perhaps I can scry Lazelan and see if he has heard of anything of this magnitude before. Perhaps he has found the *Almatraek Bright,* and can offer a suggestion as to how to lift this so we can free our people."

They disembarked once again, Sasha fairly kissing the dock once she set foot on dry land. They took the back way to the castle, approaching from the postern. The party travelled slowly, taking care to be stealthy as every little sound amid the magic-bound citizens seemed to boom in the silence. It was going to be all too easy to draw the unwanted eye of whoever was controlling the city just by being the only things that moved. Oslan did not want to give the enemy the added advantage of hearing them as well.

They made it undetected to the postern gates, and snuck past the knights' barracks. All was still there too. As they passed through the garden, Oslan was surprised to see the state of the dragon tongue tree. The ground was littered with bright orange, red and yellow leaves that the tree had begun to shed. The vines that normally hung limply now constricted the tree, and its colour was fading. Something was terribly wrong.

As he passed under its leaves, a branch seemed to move, reaching out to him, the only moving thing besides them in the kingdom. The bark split, and thick green sap started to ooze out the new crack. The tree was dying. Oslan put a reassuring hand on the tree's trunk, the side of his hand coming into contact with the slowly flowing sap, and his tattoo flared with a heat like fire. Hissing, he pulled his hand away. He would not try that again. "Your majesty, your arm!" Carn warned quietly. Oslan looked down and saw his sleeve glow under his chain mail. He hoisted the metal links and revealed the tattooed vines on his arm blazing a brilliant red. Turning to his wife, he saw that she regarded hers as well, the telltale red glow reflecting off her face. She shot him an expression of alarm. Looking around, he noted that no one else seemed to be affected. *So only those bound by the tree then,* he inferred. "Carry on," he ordered grimly, "we must get to my sisters."

Moving with their backs to the side of the main building, the king bent low and managed to peek around the corner toward the keep's main doors. He saw two armed men that were dressed in strange attire, moving back and forth in front of the entryway. Troubled, the ruler surmised that whoever the culprit was, they were inside, with his family.

"We'll have to find another way in." Oslan instructed as he pulled back to safety. Then he was struck by an idea. "Aylan, you made Sasha float up to the ship, can you aim well enough to get us in through that window?" He asked while pointing to the window of his sister's quarters above.

"Anything's possible," she replied doubtfully. "That was the first time I ever tried to lift a whole person. I had lots of space to maneuver."

"And what would you have done if you had dropped me?" Sasha asked, indignantly.

"You can swim," Aylan offered abashedly. Then to change the subject she asked: "Who would like to go first?"

"I will go," Carn volunteered.

"No," Oslan objected, "I must see to my family."

"Majesty," Carn reasoned, "If your sisters and mother are under the same influence as the rest of the people of your kingdom, then you are the only link left to the throne. They may have done this to lure you to them. By dispatching you, nothing would stand in any culprit's way of taking our land for their own. Let me go first, I beg you, I promise I will not act until I surmise that the coast is clear and you have joined me."

Oslan struggled inwardly against the feeling that it was his duty to take care of everything himself. He came to the conclusion, that Carn was right, as king, he was the least expendable of his friends gathered, however it pained him to admit it. He grudgingly nodded in allowance to Carn, giving him permission to precede him, though he felt a pang in his chest as he did so.

Carn positioned himself under the window and bowed slightly to Aylan, saying "I trust you, Your Majesty, and if I don't make it, know that I have enjoyed serving you."

Unsure of whether to laugh or cry at that, Aylan regarded her friend possibly for the last time, found her inner core of magic, and began to cast her spell.

Chapter 38
~ A Hard Life ~

As Oslan watched and silently encouraged his wife, *Come on Aylan, you can do this,* Carn began to float unsteadily upward. He reached the height of the window and peered inside, noting at once that the coast was clear. Hovering while he watched for signs of movement, he saw the princesses, Talithan, Tanyan, and the youngest, Trindalynn, all frozen like the other citizens of the kingdom. Unlike the rest though, these showed fear on their faces. He was about to look down and relay the message to the party waiting below, when the magic unceremoniously thrust him inside, and dropped him on the hard stone floor.

The crash of his armour hitting the ground rang out in the eerily quiet room. He speedily drew his sword as he jumped to his feet, heart pounding, ready for an onslaught of guards that might ensue. Mercifully, after a few moments he was able to relax as none came. He heard a sound behind him, and spun to face the window to see Oslan stepping gracefully through the frame. The king felt his heart sink and his confidence weaken as he saw the expression of terror on his sisters' faces.

One by one, the rest of the members of the party entered the antechamber of Tanyan's room through the window. There was a brief moment of doubt as to whether the burly Trembleton would fit through the small vertical space. His frizzy hair brushed the top of the window frame as his form blocked out the sunlight trying to enter. *He's not going to make it, he's too big,* thought the king in alarm, and he began to problem solve how they might get him in another way. To her credit, Aylan also saw the problem, and although the boy was carrying a fair amount of weight around his middle, he was able to just slide through, tummy and back brushing both sides of the window frame as Aylan's magic maneuvered him sideways to allow him passage. She followed last as her magic lifted her up and inside. Their party was once again complete.

Oslan watched in astonishment as Trembleton's attention immediately went to Tanyan, and the bear of a boy raced to her side. He hugged her unyielding stone-like form in a desperate embrace while whispering her name over and over. "Oh, Tanyan, Tanyan, I promise I'll find a way to free you, sweet angel."

Up in arms about this display of contact with his favourite sister, Oslan was about to order his friend to release her, when an amazing thing happened. A single tear ran down Tanyan's cheek as Trembleton released her and knelt before her. "No, weep not, my angel, I am still here." He said while gently wiping the tear away.

Oslan was finding it hard to put two and two together. "Wait, Trembleton, *you*... and *my sister*?"

Trembleton smiled up weakly at the king, "Since the night your father fell ill after the ball, Sire."

"This is amazing Oslan!" Aylan intoned excitedly.

"You're telling me," the king replied in a daze.

"Oslan!" Aylan reprimanded sharply. Oslan's attention snapped back to the problem at hand, and he regarded his queen-mage as she went on. "This answers some of our questions. Even though our subjects seem frozen like stone, they *are* still alive and they *are* aware. This means that there is hope of undoing this travesty."

Trembleton smiled up gratefully at her

announcement. "Whatever I can do to help you, Your Majesty, I will do."

"Then let's get to the armoury," She replied.

"It is probably guarded," Carn reasoned.

"That won't be a problem," Sasha interjected, "for we will be invisible."

Aylan's hand went to a small pouch at her belt and loosened the mouth of it. She upended it and poured a series of little brown balls into her palm.

"Your Grace, not to question your magical abilities, but those look like they're made out of dirt," Thorn objected. "What do you want us to do with those?"

"They're invisibility pills" Sasha informed them as Aylan began to give one to each of them.

"We will need that pitcher of water. Trust me, they don't go down easily," Aylan warned as Trembleton got the water from the nightstand. "They don't taste the best either."

Aylan plugged her nose and showed them how to place the pill on their tongues, and drink from the pitcher to help swallow them down. She handed the water back to her knight and the queen disappeared before their eyes. "Whoa!" Thorn intoned under his breath. He immediately popped his pill into his mouth, forgetting to pinch his nose against the taste. He began to sputter and hack as he desperately grabbed for the pitcher to wash it down. He managed to swallow the pill and disappear as Aylan had, but the poor boy could still be heard adamantly cursing about the foul flavour.

"If it's to work," reported Sasha, "you must be silent, otherwise, your filthy mouth will give us away!"

"But it *is* filthy, that's the problem! Honestly, you've never tasted anything so awful in your entire life. This is even worse than the time that mother was away and father thought he would try his hand at cooking!" His voice grew sad at the memory, and Oslan's heart went out to the poor lad.

"Right", Bowregard announced, making sure to pinch his nose between his fingers before he swallowed his pill. He disappeared. One by one the others consumed Aylan's little brown tablets, and soon the room appeared empty save for the three princesses frozen in time.

Chapter 39
~ About Face ~

Oslan ordered Carn to inch the door open slowly so as not to attract the unwanted attention of possible guards. Except for the two marching back and forth in front of the keep's double doors though, Oslan hadn't seen a one. He speculated that if no one could move, whoever had done this probably figured that they were safe. His blood began to boil at how low they had brought his kingdom. *I will deal with these villains myself,* he thought menacingly. Their advantage was that Oslan knew who they were looking for, and the enemy didn't seem to be well guarded. He relaxed his hands that were balled into fists of rage.

"Watch your feet and armour, they will still make a terrific amount of sound as you move." Aylan warned.

"We should remove it." Oslan decided.

"But Sire, to go into the fire with naught to protect us?" Carn questioned, "Is that wise?"

"We are invisible and will have the element of surprise," he affirmed. "The armour comes off, but keep your weapons," he ordered. The next few minutes passed with Oslan's heart beating loudly in his own chest. The metal was so loud to remove, and Aylan was right, each time its parts hit together, the sound echoed through the room as if someone had struck a gong. The noise put them all on edge, but still, no one came to confront them.

"Perhaps we should push it all under the bed," Bow suggested, "then if it becomes visible before we are ready, and someone glances in, it may take longer to be discovered."

"Good man," was Oslan's reply as he pushed his armour under the great four post bed.

Oslan spared one last look at his sisters, and then he and his party, now able to move silently without their clanging armour, made their way into the empty hallway toward the armoury.

*   *   *

In the throne room, the baroness, Aurastia, purred once again to the other mage. "Oh Zaltreous, worry not, they are lifeless and we now own this kingdom." Elsa, the queen mother, and several of the nobles that had been in attendance during the king's absence had been unceremoniously moved to the far corner of the large hall. There they leaned against one wall as they stood and sat in their various rictus poses. Zaltreous paced back and forth in front of them, stopping every few steps to eye them cautiously. Their unmoving watching eyes made him feel uneasy.

"I just don't like that they can see our faces. If something should happen, there is no question that we two are responsible for this." Zaltreous grumbled. He didn't like to second guess this stunning beauty, it always made her cross, and he had seen first-hand that it was not fun to cross her. He had brought her fortress down and she had grumbled about it during the whole three day journey here. Still, he couldn't help but feel like he was a tool to her, much as her servant Flanx was.

"And *what* could possibly happen?" She asked, voice rising slightly. "You wanted revenge on this kingdom, and we have taken it! Come sit by my side on your rightful throne, and be content." Her voice was smooth honey again.

"The king could return, for one thing." He voiced.

"Ha ha ha ha ha," she laughed, "and when he does, we will be ready. I have two of my men guarding the only door into the keep. Believe me, he won't get in without us knowing."

"It would not be wise to underestimate Oslan, my dear," Zaltreous pushed, "Let me remind you that it was him who was able to capture me in the first place. He is a cunning sort," he revealed bitterly.

"Come now, Zaltreous. Any man, even a powerful mage like you, might not have been able to stand up to such a large group of warriors," She placated.

"Yes, but I even had the book!" He warned.

"And now you have me!" She threw at him fiercely, while her talon-like hands gripped the arms of the throne upon which she sat. Recomposing herself, she continued. "I grow weary of this conversation. If they bother you so much turn them around, or take a tapestry from the wall and cover them up."

Zaltreous sat back crossly in his throne, realizing not for the first time, that she was trying to placate him as one would a child. He began to form a plan in his head to take the book and leave, but his thoughts were stopped in their tracks as she turned to him and smiled an all too knowing and dangerous smile.

Chapter 40
~ A Kick To Boot ~

As they crept down the hallway, every sound from each footfall's accidently dragged heel seemed to resonate off the walls, making Oslan cringe. Still, no one came to face them. They turned the last corner that would give them access to the armoury. Oslan stopped dead in his tracks, causing the next person to walk into him. Luckily, whoever it was had been cunning enough to keep their mouth shut upon impact. There were still two guards posted outside the doors, but these wore no livery of the castle. They were the interloper's men. One tall and thin, the other shorter and fat, they each stood at attention with a spear in one hand.

Oslan began to move his band once again down the hallway, and noticed with some relief that the armoury doors hung wide open. They began to pass between the guards without making a sound. Oslan held his breath as he passed by unnoticed and felt elation once he was inside.

He could hear voices from inside the next room where they needed to be, and its doors barred the way. *This is where they all must be,* Oslan realized, trying to devise a way to form a castle sentry with so few men. It would be difficult to enter without them noticing the movement of the huge doors. The king began to develop an idea while the others continued to make their way silently into the armoury, until one of the guards at the door spoke.

"Do you smell something?" The thin guard asked as he wrinkled his nose.

"Oh, come off it!" the second guard responded, "The first one who smelt it, dealt it."

"Nah," replied the first guard, with genuine interest now, "It don't smell like rotten wind, it

211

smells...of fear."

"The only thing *I'm* afraid of is your odour in this enclosed space," the second fat guard retorted matter-of-factly.

Ignoring him, the first guard thrust his spear at the apparently empty space in front of him. Sasha had seen the spear flying towards her moments before it happened, and unquestioningly, she dropped to her stomach on the ground. The spear cut silently through the air above her where moments before her face had been.

As a reaction, Oslan and Carn drew their swords, each making an unmistakably loud ringing *shing*. The fat guard turned into the room at the sound, now on the alert. "Who's there?" He challenged.

Behind him, Oslan could see a coil of rope rise up off of its peg on the wall, and come down over the guard, pinning his arms to his side. A knot formed in the rope, which seemed to tie itself, but Oslan recognized the skilled work of Bowregard. Before the man could cry out further, Oslan rushed over and used the hilt of his sword to knock out the fat guard with a blow to the back of his head. Meanwhile, the tall man that was left was thrusting wildly with his spear in all directions around him. Oslan recognized Aylan's voice as he heard the word "Fuer!" *Fire!* and the wooden shaft on the guard's spear burst into flames, singeing his hand and causing him to drop his weapon. He screamed, and now unarmed, started to run down the hall away from the armoury.

"Quick, before he can alert the others!" Oslan cried. He heard questioning voices and the sound of many chairs scraping against the stone floor as people stood within the war room. *Too late.* "We are going to need a distraction," he ordered.

"We've got this," stated Thorn as he stepped back into the hallway. Nocking an invisible arrow in his practiced hands, he shot down the hall. His arrow found its mark in the back of the running guard, dropping him to the cold flagstone floor.

"I'm with you," Trembleton's voice came from behind his right shoulder.

"Wait, you can't do any good like that, they won't see you." Sasha said. She picked up a nearby brazier and judging from their voices, threw the ashy contents their way. The cloud of soot that rose into the air was impressive, and effective. Before them now stood two figures covered in black and white ash that sputtered and coughed.

Sasha handed the brazier to Trembleton and backed against the wall as the war room doors were flung opened, and a dozen men ran out. Seeing their companion tied and slumped on the floor, and two strange sooty beings in the doorway, one member of the guards put two and two together, and yelled "Hey, you there, stop!"

With admirable skill, Trembleton threw the heavy metal brazier at the closest charging opponent, hitting him square in the face. The loud crunch from the impact that knocked the pursuer down was a tell-tale sign of a broken nose. The others stopped charging in surprise as the man with a now crooked bloody nose screamed in rage. Trembleton said "Sorry mate, you probably should have ducked from that one," and took off with Thorn down the hall. The other men who had stopped to help their wounded commander were ordered to leave him be and go get the scum, with the threat of Aurastia's wrath should they fail. The injured man slowly got to his feet, muttering, "What a mess this is." Checking his face for blood, he spared a long glance at the unconscious guard, and kicked his boot hard, ordering "Wake up!" When the prone man didn't stir, the commander returned to the war room to consult his map of the castle.

Luckily, Trembleton's quick thinking, and the man's unkindness towards his fellow officer had given Aylan, Sasha, Carn, Bow, and the king enough time to slip behind the tapestry and into the secret passageway. Oslan was fairly sure that they had made it completely unnoticed.

Chapter 41
~ Intrusion ~

They reached the workroom as the invisibility pills wore off, luckily with no sign of pursuit. Entering, Oslan heard Aylan call out "Fuer," *Fire,* and flames on the wicks of all of the candles around the room flickered to life at once.

The illumination revealed a chamber with wall to wall shelves of vials, pouches, pots, potions, and jars. Each one had a neat label, and stood organized without a thing out of place. In the center of the room was a high wooden table with stools around it. In the center of the table there was another smaller brazier, with a small cooking pot suspended above it. A mortar and pestle, and several spoons were neatly laid out for mixing and measuring ingredients. On the back wall, there leaned a huge four foot mirror within a gilded frame.

"What is this place?" Bowregard exclaimed in awe.

Carn just shook his head in confusion. "Oslan," he asked, "how long has this been here?"

"Since the castle was built," Oslan replied almost apologetically. "Its secret has been passed down from king to king, and kept from everyone to protect it. This is the royal mage's workroom. It once belonged to Lazelan, and now belongs to the queen."

"Are there *more* passageways like the one that brought us here?" Bow asked, the idea striking him like an arrow shot from Thorn's gigantic bow. "Perhaps we can use them to move around the castle unnoticed."

Oslan struggled for a long time, balancing the idea of disclosing to more people the secrets that were bestowed on him by his beloved father.

"Secrets were meant to be kept, otherwise they'd be called gossip," his father had been fond of saying.

But these men had grown with him, fought by his side, and he trusted them with his life. His heart twisted sourly at the thought of disappointing the memory of his da, taken too soon from him. He had been trusted with so much, and so far in his short reign as king, he had divulged all of his family's secrets to those he thought he could trust. This was the one last thing he had that he could one day pass down to his own son should he have one. Having thought that, he realized that he may never have a chance to have an heir if they couldn't get out of this alive.

As Bow had hedged wisely, this may be the best chance they would have to regain his kingdom. Perhaps it would be their only chance. The element of surprise can be very powerful and give an underdog the best fighting chance. Ormond had taught them all that; he and his brothers-in-arms that waited expectantly as the silence panned out between them. Oslan silently apologised to his father, and asked the brightness to guide him as he revealed his family's last secret.

"There are more hidden passageways that lead from one room to another so that we may pass into the throne room unnoticed." Oslan confided, "It is sometimes inconvenient to have to wade through a throng of courtiers, and always show decorum when walking through one's own home. However, we rarely use the passages, they are mainly there in case of a siege, in order to get the royal family out safely and unnoticed."

"If I were to invade a castle," Carn admitted, "it would be there that I would take up command. It is a central location and holds the thrones, the seats of power." The thought of Zaltreous sitting on his father's throne angered the king, and he resolved to be the evil mage's undoing.

While the men had been talking, Aylan had been conferring with Sasha as to the whereabouts of Lazelan. Sasha had been keeping tabs on him in her trances, so that Aylan could find him when she needed to. She had also informed them that their scrying packets had been thwarted, which allowed them to scry within the walls once more. Oslan took note that she was ready, quieted the room, and stood back to watch her work her magic.

Approaching the tall mirror, she waved a slender arm over the surface and began her incantation in Almatrae. "Vearta uta da Ey seche ot isa. Vearta so Wornad Embralic. Vearta Lazelan." *Reveal that which I seek to see. Reveal the Embralic Desert. Reveal Lazelan.*

The surface of the mirror shimmered, like ripples of water on a pond after a goose touches down from flight. As the small waves lessened and faded, the image of the workroom was replaced with Lazelan's face swimming into view. Droplets of sweat beaded his forehead and he absentmindedly pulled a handkerchief from a pocket and dabbed at the moisture on his brow. His shirt clung to his tall frame, slicked with sweat, which he plucked away from his body.

He was talking to a beautiful woman, tall with dark skin, who sat on a high backed chair of intricately carved spiraling alabaster. She was dressed in a light flowing fabric that was simple, yet elegant. Two dark skinned men, naked to the waist, stood on either side of her, fanning her with the fronds of some wide leafed fern.

As Aylan began to scry the scene, the woman's attention was pulled in their direction, and it appeared as though she were staring right at them.

Lazelan's face burst into a wide grin, but one of the men standing near the woman on the throne pulled a knife from a sheath in his boot and took a step forward. The woman held a hand up, and the man stopped in his tracks. The expression on her face hardened, and her eyes seemed to bore into the king. The feeling was uncanny, and forced Oslan to take a step back in unease. He looked to his mage and asked, "She can't see us, can she?"

Aylan replied in a disturbed voice, "If I didn't know it wasn't possible, I'd swear she was."

With a serious face, the woman waved a hand as if in greeting, and suddenly the tiny castle workroom was filled with her smooth voice. "Kil prat ot rohagah so halitah nula so fai, Xinavane?" *Who dares to invade the privacy of the princess, Xinavane?*

The strange language rose and fell on the king's ears, and at once, he saw Aylan's harried appearance change. She lowered her hands to her sides, straightened perceptively, and raised her chin, taking her most regal stance. She replied in a calm voice, the carrying voice Oslan recognized as the one she used to address her subjects. "Xa tax Ey, Fait Aylan, nula Endalwynndale. Ey realpe lan so kliptahkia, Fai, xa taxiyat eyt aol taelah est kai, Lazelan, Ey taxiyat actah ot setev." *It is I, Queen Aylan, of Endalwynndale. I apologize for the intrusion, Princess, it was my good friend and teacher, Lazelan, I was trying to find*

Oslan could not speak a word of Almatrae, but he prided himself on being able to read people very well. This skill helped him to best deal with nobles or others he interacted with. He could see that the woman in the mirror was considering Aylan's words, weighing them. She looked to Lazelan, who nodded his acknowledgement, or perhaps verification, and the countenance of the whole room changed. Oslan hadn't realized he had been holding his breath until he felt it rush out of him as the woman replied to Aylan in a much friendlier tone.

"Liyat kasdi oay takiyat rau box, Zai, lan tay postik seteviyat oay." *Then consider him lost no more, Highness, for you have found him.*

Chapter 42
~ Bark Worse Than Its Bite ~

Lazelan exchanged a few quick words with the princess across the room while Aylan explained to the others who they had stumbled upon. After a shallow bow to the princess, Lazelan came closer to the surface of the mirror to speak more privately with his old friends.

"Greetings Sire, Highness, I hope all is well." He said while he made the kingdom's salute.

"I'm afraid all is not well, my old friend," replied Oslan solemnly, and proceeded to fill in his father's former mage on both their success at finding the circlet, and what they had found upon returning to their kingdom. Lazelan turned to the princess of the desert tribes and told her of the state of the citizens of Endalwynndale. She at once came closer and asked Aylan some questions for clarification in an alarmed voice. "Kaae kaet piix mas? Kaae xa postik aweya?" *Does their skin move? Does it have colour?*

Frustrated by the language barrier, and impatient to be doing something useful, Oslan urged Aylan to translate. "What is wrong, what is she saying?"

Aylan translated the questions and Oslan clarified, for he had been close when Trembleton had embraced his sister's frozen form. "Her skin was hard, pale, and immovable, as if turned to stone. No breeze, nor touch could ripple a hair on her head," he replied surely.

As Aylan relayed the message, Xinavane strode back to her throne and with a double clap of her hands, sent three servants running to do her bidding. While she waited for their return, Lazelan informed Oslan that though he had not yet found the book of counter spells, the *Almatraek Bright*, he had made his way through death defying obstacles to the palace in the Embralic Desert, where Xinavane, one of the contributors to the book lived. She had personally scribed a few of her own spells into the book, and perhaps with some luck, she will have an idea of what this treachery was.

Behind Lazelan, the three servants returned, each with a heavy book bound in leather. Without any sort of visible command issued, a fourth servant immediately knelt in front of Xinavane, and took up a position on hands and knees like a table. The first servant with a book laid it upon his flat back, and the princess began to frantically leaf through the pages. After glancing quickly at a few spells in succession, she called "Rau!" *No!* The empty handed servant stepped forward to retrieve the book he had brought. He bustled away once again with it, as the next servant laid his offering on the back of the semi-prone man. This time, after looking over the first few spells, she flipped directly to the middle of the book, causing her "table" to grunt under the pressure, and affording him a glare from the princess. She turned the next page over and exclaimed "Fuele jo umek nae, Ey postik seteviyat xa!" *Brightness be with us, I have found it!*

Oslan had begun pacing back and forth from one end of Aylan's small workroom to the other, while far away across the world, Lazelan discussed the spell with the princess. Impatient and helpless, Oslan would every once in a while, stop to read some of the labels on her various vials and jars, then resume his pacing while he waited. Eventually, Lazelan thanked the princess and approached the mirror once more.

"It is a spell from the *Almatraek Dim* alright," he confirmed. "But luckily you have the antidote with you. The bad news is that retrieving it is going to hurt...a lot." Lazelan hesitated before going on. "In fact, it might even kill you."

"If it saves my people, I would make that sacrifice," Oslan replied immediately, returning to face the mirror.

"I know Sire," Lazelan replied with a quick troubled glance at Aylan, "but are you prepared to sacrifice your wife?"

Oslan took a step closer to his mage, and put a protective arm around her, allowing his fingers to intertwine with hers. He felt her delicate hand gently squeeze his palm in support of whatever he decided. Worry creased his brow as he thought about all the trials he and Aylan had overcome to be together. It seemed as though as soon as they were able to take a step forward, fate transpired against them, forcing them back. He sighed heavily, sporting the weight of the world and asked "What needs to be done?"

Lazelan looked apologetically to the couple, and explained that the princess had found the counter-spell amongst her writings, but that names here were not the same, so not all of it was clear.

"To crack the stone, you must awaken the tree." Lazelan said cryptically, "the tree that flares at sundown and dawn, and shares the name of the scaled beast whose spirit resides within. Only a love that blazes like the fire of the creature will let loose its scorching breath. To shatter the bark, you must first break the vine, its fierce fiery blast will the stone then unbind." Lazelan's voice resonated through the small room, till its echoes faded from the walls. The space stood silent while they all puzzled out the possible meanings of the magic that could bring their trapped loved ones back to them.

"It's the dragon tongue tree. Highnesses, it

burned you fiercely when you touched its bark. It's got to be that." Bowregard intoned as he broke the silence.

"He is right, I have seen it." Sasha added, "But the tree is dying. We've got to hurry, before all is lost."

"That is not all!" warned Lazelan through the mirror's shining surface, "Both or one of you must stay with the tree, or the dragon's spirit will run rampant, an unstoppable force overrunning your kingdom. Only when the tree is resealed will your people truly be safe. Until then, those that open its shell must not break contact, lest it die completely. Your life force will keep the tree alive while the beast is at its work. It is an ancient sort of magic that won't stop until the spirit is once again locked up, and licking the sky with its leaves."

Lazelan gave Aylan a look, urging her to remember her teachings. She knew that a spell could borrow the life force from other unsuspecting living things around it to boost its magic. She also knew that if her energy was used up, she might never cast again, and that if her or Oslan's life force was drained completely, one or both of them would die. Oslan saw the fear etched on her face and felt her shudder within the circle of his arm, and he held her closer still.

Chapter 43
~ A Need For Greed ~

"I suppose our next move is to get to the tree to free the kingdom," Carn offered. "What are we waiting for? We must make haste." Glad to finally have a plan, Oslan gratefully started to move across the room, finally put into action.

"Not so fast!" Sasha ordered, "We mustn't free them until after we have taken care of Zaltreous and his tall dark-haired companion."

"Nonsense, if we free the town folk first it will cause a distraction, and we'll have more knights at our disposal to help us." Bowregard reasoned.

"Good man!" Oslan complimented as he clapped his friend on the shoulder for his quick thinking and headed for the door, now relieved that he could be doing something useful.

Panicked, Sasha drew herself up to her full height, and scolded Oslan much more loudly than she ever raised her musical voice. "With all due respect, King Oslan, stop your hot-headed foolishness and listen to reason for a second!" Stunned into silence, all eyes turned to the normally quiet woman that now stood with fists balled up on her hips and a look on her face much akin to a mother's when one has tracked mud across her freshly cleaned floor.

"Am I your seer for nothing?" She questioned him sternly. "Right now the townsfolk are right where the usurpers want them. They are safe, and Zaltreous and this other mage woman have been lulled into a sense of security. If we release the townsfolk now, the two mages will rain down fire upon everyone and everything in panic. I have seen it. They will kill many of your subjects, and we will have to deal with confused people as they come out of the stony spell. They will want answers, and will try to detain us until they get them, and then nothing will have been gained. Not only that, but Sire, if the worst happens, and you and the queen die while trying to save the people, then there will be no one to challenge or try them for their treason on the throne. We must head to the throne room first with the circlet, and we must hurry, for if the tree dies before we can get to it, then all is lost."

Oslan felt horror struck and ashamed at the thought of his people dying because he hadn't taken the time to consider every angle the way his father and Ormond had taught him. He would have rushed in blindly and their deaths would have been on his hands. Now it was his turn to shudder. He stepped toward Sasha, taking her upper arms in his hands, and looked sternly into her face.

"I beg you to forgive my hastiness Sasha," he told her, "Of course you are right, thank you for putting things into perspective for me." Then, turning back to his knights and mage, he reflected, "We need a plan, and quick."

"I might have one," Aylan responded, "but first, a question. Lazelan?" Aylan asked as she turned back to the mirror that still held his image, "Tell me something about the circlet. If we should perchance get it upon one of the mages' heads, what is stopping them from simply taking it off and tossing it aside, rendering it useless?"

"That is the beauty of the circlet," replied Lazelan, "The magic only comes to life when touched by a mage. Once the metal touches the flesh of someone that has the gift of magic, only another mage may remove it. That doesn't happen very often, since the mage who removed it would then lose their power."

"But I don't understand," said Carn, puzzled,

"How was Aylan able to retrieve the circlet from the cave?"

"After what happened with the packets hidden in your armour, I wasn't about to touch a magic item that could drain my energy," Aylan confessed, "I first wrapped the fabric of my sleeve around my hand and hoped for the best. The metal never touched me. This time though, I think I might have to actually wear the vial thing. I have an idea that just might work."

"No way," Oslan contradicted as soon as the words were out of her mouth. "I will not have you don something that will leave you defenseless. If your plan goes awry there are no other mages here that could remove it for you."

"Oslan," she reasoned with him, "tell me what you know of these two mages we are about to face."

"They are powerful and dangerous," he answered at once.

"Yes, what else?" She encouraged, rolling her eyes at his stubbornness.

"They are power hungry," Bow stated matter-of-factly, "Why else would they try to take over a whole kingdom?"

"Good, and what is the utmost symbol of power in a kingdom? What makes people recognize someone as the ruler?" She pushed.

"The royal crown." They all said together.

"Right, so what would be the most satisfactory way for them to take our kingdom from us?" She asked finally.

"For them to strip us of our circlets, and then wear the crowns themselves," Oslan thought aloud.

"Yes," Aylan agreed, "When I walk into the throne room wearing it at your side Oslan, they won't be able to resist taking it from me."

Oslan felt his mouth twitch up into a half smile at the genius of his queen. A feeling of warmth flooded him as he fell in love with her all over again. Brightness be with them, he loved this woman. He had sworn to protect her, and he was going to have to, for when she placed the circlet upon her head, she would be as defenseless as a babe.

Chapter 44
~ Crowning Around ~

"Wish me luck!" Aylan said to Lazelan's image as Oslan slipped an arm around her waist. The others in the small room shuffled uncomfortably and suddenly found something particularly interesting by their feet to look at as the king gently pulled his queen into an embrace. Kissing her tenderly, Oslan felt a rush of desperation to keep her safe. He had waited his whole life to feel this way about someone, and it never ceased to amaze him that this perfect creature for some reason felt the same way about him. She was charming, witty, beautiful, and talented, making him feel inadequate at best. He would not let any harm come to her, he would keep her safe or die trying.

Clinging to that thought, he slowly pulled away from her and slipped his hand into the satchel that hung at her waist. He extracted the circlet and regarded it. It was a shining example of impressive craftsmanship, with spirals of worked metal that rose and fell, looped and intertwined into an intricate pattern that converged upon one red ruby at the front. It looked delicate, but weighed heavily upon him. He sighed deeply, not liking the plan, but not seeing any better way to do this.

"Ready?" He asked.

She removed the delicate gleaming band that now always adorned her forehead. She laid it upon the table, took a deep breath and nodded at him, closing her eyes to steel herself against whatever sensations the circlet would bring. Oslan was painfully gentle as he laid the wretched thing upon her hair, snugging it down over her brow. She at once swooned under its insignificant weight, and he caught her in both arms around her waist, supporting her as she regained her senses. He could feel her shaking like a leaf against him as she opened her eyes.

"Oslan," she whispered without any strength to her voice.

"I am here," he told her, "what do you feel? Does it hurt? Are you in pain, my love?"

She shook her head slowly, and began to stand on her own. "I can feel my energy still within me, but it has been locked away from me. I know it's there, but I can't get to it. It feels like a cruel child who has stolen something of value from one smaller than he, and dangles it just out of reach of his victim. I am as weak and powerless to stop it as that little child. All I can do is reach, but it is ever out of my ability to embrace it. It is awful and uncanny." She confessed as tears began to slip down her face.

Oslan felt his heart break at the sight. *This is ridiculous, I never should have allowed it!* "Lazelan, please, you have to do some-", but his pleading words died on the air as he regarded the mirror that now only showed their reflection.

*   *   *

Oslan had commanded their group to split up. He had left Sasha in the workroom to hide in case all was lost, with instructions to guide Lazelan to them if he should find a way to scry her, and their party did not return. If it came to that, he knew Lazelan would come, and that he would bring help. Bow and Carn had been ordered to try to enter the throne room the traditional way, through the main double doors, which would create a diversion. Meanwhile, he and Aylan would attempt to catch the evil mages unaware by sneaking into the throne room through the secret passageway that lay behind the royal family's thrones.

Oslan's band had slipped out of the secret passageway into the war room to find it empty, and the mess in the armoury exactly as they had left it. The unconscious guard still lay breathing deeply against one wall. Fully visible now, the group rounded the door into the empty hallway. Breaking apart, the king and queen left the others to plan their entrance to the throne room, and made their way to Oslan's mother's chambers.

They entered, not bothering to knock, as they knew no one would answer. It was from here that they would gain access to the second passageway. Oslan moved to the large fireplace, and regarded a statuette of a lion with wings standing proudly on the mantle. Stroking its head, he let his index finger trace down its snout until it reached the tip of the lion's nose. He pushed his finger inward, and the nose moved. He heard the familiar sound of stone grinding against stone as a panel at the back of the fireplace opened to reveal a hallway beyond.

"Wait," Aylan called to him as he prepared to duck into the filthy opening. He turned to see her open the tall wardrobe his mother and father used to share before his passing. "If we are to do this, we must look the part. I need a dress, and you need a crown." He watched as she selected one of his mother's dresses, a regal thing made of layers of lace and ruffles at the sleeves and down the front of the skirt. It was deep purple and had a very high neck line. He turned to let her disrobe and redress, and reached into a panel at the back of the wardrobe that contained his father's favourite crown. It was rather plain, but it was the one Oslan remembered seeing him in the most. It was no wonder his mother kept it here, it must give her a myriad of recollections the way it did for him. He could see watermarks across the brow where presumably, his mother had stood holding it, crying over the loss of her husband.

He used his thumb to gently rub away the salty blemishes, and then used his sleeve to rid the crown of the oils from his thumb. He could not imagine life without Aylan. They were a team, a pair, and he could not fathom what his strong mother had gone through, was still going through, now that his father was gone. He stood for a moment, fondly admiring the crown in its simplicity, before placing it upon his head. It was a little big, resting on the tops of his ears, but in this situation, he didn't think Zaltreous would notice.

He turned at the sound of Aylan beckoning him over. "I need your help doing this up." She stated, her back to him, gown gaping open down her spine as loose chords dangled from a pair of eyelets at her waist.

At a loss, he explained "Er, I really don't know where to begin or how to do this up properly."

"You have gotten me out of gowns like this quite a few times since we've been married!" she exclaimed, exasperated, "Figure it out!"

"Yes," he agreed as his fingers began to fumble with lacing the chord, "and I sincerely hope I will get another chance to do so." He admitted while remembering the last time fondly, and giving her a roguish look over her shoulder in the mirror before her.

"Oslan!" she hissed, scandalized. "I am in your mother's dress."

"And you look beautiful," he admitted freely. She crossed her arms across her chest and glared at him for almost a full twenty seconds in the mirror before the edges of her mouth started to turn up. Feeling rather smug, he grinned back. He knew she couldn't stay mad at him for long. He finished the lacing with a knot and stepped back to look at her.

"You look regal," he decided with an affirming nod. He took her hand and led her to the large white mantle.

"Ready?" he asked, half hoping she would say no and they could stay here safe and happy together a little while longer. She nodded, resigned to see their plan to its end. The pair passed through the sooty fireplace and into the passageway beyond, pausing only long enough to light a torch when the stone door slid shut behind them.

Chapter 45
~ A Crowning Achievement ~

They almost succeeded. What they hadn't counted on was Flanx, at his station in front of the wall near the thrones in case the villains needed him. He stood with his back to the gigantic red tapestry that hung as a backsplash to the thrones. This tapestry depicted Endalwynndale's beautiful dragon tongue tree, and the marriage ceremony of King Eurilas to Queen Elsa. Many of the nobles had been tickled to have been able to pick out their families represented as being in attendance that day within the weave of threads.

What Oslan hadn't known was that Flanx's post on the other side of the tapestry lay directly in front of the secret passage. The king had extinguished the flame of the torch in the last few feet of their journey. A brighter section of the tapestry illuminated the end of the corridor as it allowed faint light to spill through from the room beyond. He could smell the familiar dusty scent of the fabric, and waited for the sounds of Carn and Bow entering at the other end of the room. He drew his sword slowly in preparation and cringed at the loud grinding noise it made coming out of its sheath. In stealthy situations, he always worried that the sound would echo loudly and someone would hear it. No one ever did, until today.

On the other side of the cloth, Flanx not only heard the telltale sound of a sword being drawn, but listened more closely, and discovered he could hear the nervous breathing of people trying to steel themselves. He silently moved to the thrones and motioned to his noble mistress there, so that when the sounds of battle were finally heard outside the throne room's double doors, and Oslan took the last step, pushing aside the tapestry to admit them into the hall, they did so under the scrutiny of three pairs of expectant and glaring eyes. Oslan's heart sank as he knew all might now be lost.

"Oslan," Zaltreous identified the king, an amused edge to his voice, "And his little mage too. My, you look all grown up since I saw you last."

"Enough!" barked Aurastia, her cadence no longer soft velvet. It was then that they all heard Bow yell loudly from the hallway, "Carn, duck!" followed by a heavy *thwok!* The right side of the double doors swung open to reveal a guard pinned through his middle to the heavy oak by one of Bow's arrows. He groaned as his blood stained the wood's grain.

Oslan and Aylan exchanged a look of surprise as their two companions entered the hall. Carn now carried Oslan's shield though they had left it with their armour. *They must have looped back around to get it,* Oslan thought triumphantly, *it will give us another advantage.*

"Move them over there with the others, so our attention will need not be divided," Aurastia commanded.

Oslan felt his legs bear less and less weight until finally, his feet came off the ground. He held onto his sword through the surprise of getting whisked across the room, and a moment later, his stomach lurched as he was unceremoniously dropped and the magic withdrew. He fell, landing in a crouched position on one foot and one knee. His father's ill-fitting crown tumbled to the ground, clanging loudly. Oslan watched for a moment as it circled on its rim, the way a coin will on a table top before lying flat. It rolled around and around faster and faster, it's metal edge coming closer and closer to the ground as it seemed to gain momentum. It finally came to a stop and he retrieved it with one hand, placing it once again on his head. Looking up at his two foes, he rose slowly, still brandishing Skirdkhen.

"You have tried to take my kingdom from me. You have failed," he informed them levelly.

"On the contrary!" Zaltreous crowed in jubilation, "We have taken your people, we have taken your palace and we have taken your thrones! All that is left for us to take now are your crowns!"

Oslan saw Aylan make a quick movement from the corner of his eye. *No, don't draw attention to yourself!* He thought desperately, and readied himself to jump in front of her if they made a move to blast her with magic.

"What have you got there?" Aurastia questioned as she beckoned Aylan forward.

"Nothing," Aylan replied in a slightly too innocent voice.

"Flanx, go and get whatever she is hiding." Aurastia ordered, then to Aylan, "You do know you are powerless to stop us, why would you even try?"

She doesn't know how right she is, Oslan thought as he watched the old man shuffle towards his helpless wife. Gritting his teeth, he comforted himself with thinking that at least they had sent the servant instead of outright attacking her.

Flanx reached the queen and circled her, as the prince willed himself not to move. The servant reached out to take the hidden crown from her hands. He thought better of it though, and reported to Aurastia instead.

"It appears to be a crown." His rusty voice sounded through the hall.

"The Circlet of Dalenden!" Zaltreous responded reverently. "How did you get it?" he asked.

"How is not important," replied Aurastia. "Flanx, what is taking so long, bring it to me."

The servant gave Aurastia a withering look, and Oslan thought for a moment that the man was tired of being spoken to so rudely. He could only imagine what it was like for this man to have worked for her, especially given her cruel nature and quickness to kill. He reckoned that it would be like living within a den of lions that could strike out any time they decided they were hungry.

The old man hesitated for a moment longer and then reached out his hand to take it again. At that moment, he stumbled on his long robe. He fell into Aylan, making her throw her hands out in front of her to break her fall should she go down. She managed to keep her footing, but the crown was now exposed.

Chapter 46
~ Elements of a Good Fight ~

As Flanx struggled unsteadily to his feet, Zaltreous moved like lightning. He hurled an invisible force across the room to knock the old man back. "Enough of this incompetent bumbling!" Zaltreous incanted another spell and a second later the crown flew from Aylan's hands and skidded to a halt at the foot of the throne's dais.

"Thank you, darling." Aurastia once again purred at the black haired mage, now placated. "That was a very dangerous move, Highness," she observed, "and a very stupid one," she concluded, turning to Zaltreous.

His triumphant grin from a moment ago was wiped clean off his face.

"You see," she continued, as if explaining to a child, "While she held that, she was powerless, which is probably why she didn't cast on us immediately upon entering the room. The Circlet of Dalenden can only be removed by a mage, and now it has been, relinquishing all her powers back to her." As Aurastia spoke to him, her voice grew harsher and harsher. "Make yourself useful, and find a spell in the book to stop her."

As a kicked dog will, he lashed out to bite someone else. "Flanx, perhaps you could bring it upon your very elderly self to bring us their real crowns now. I suggest you move with haste, or you will be sliding across the floor in the same manner as that circlet!" Flanx reached up and quickly plucked both of the royal couple's crowns from their heads, stumbling again as he began shuffling back to his mistress.

As soon as Flanx fell, everyone spun into action. Zaltreous, who had been frantically turning pages in the book, let out a gleeful "Ah-ha!" and began casting loudly in Almatrae. Bowregard drew an arrow from his quiver but was unable to get a clean shot due to a rush of chilled air that Oslan felt swoop by him. Aylan spoke quickly in a clear ringing voice, both her and Zaltreous in a battle to be the first to finish and strike against the other. Oslan moved around his mage and gained a clear line of attack on the motionless Aurastia, who still sat shocked on the throne.

"Kaeja nula kusayt taekiel, faktomas oay jel!" *Gust of winter's breath, drive him back!* Aylan's voice cried above the icy wind that now howled around them and flew across the room with the strength of a derecho toward Zaltreous and the pedestal holding the *Almatraek Dim*. The frigid gale force wind whipped Zaltreous backward, away from the book whose pages were fluttering wildly in the blast fit to rip them from the book's spine. The mage hit the back wall of the throne room hard enough to knock all the wind out of him, interrupting his ability to finish the incantation. No sooner had he hit the wall then Aurastia, who had finally started to act, stood and raised a sure and steady palm toward the charging Oslan.

Carn started forward to collect the fallen Zaltreous, sword and shield brandished in front of him. For his part, Flanx who had been flung down in his pile of robes, had righted himself back on his feet, and now moved with the speed of a younger man as he tried to intercept the king. He started muttering something under his breath, attempting to throw down the crowns on his way to free his hands for the tackle. Aurastia now shifted her weight nervously as Oslan drew nearer, her eyes slid toward her servant and she repeatedly pressed her palm out toward the king with a confused look on her face.

She looks like a squire with a peace-bonded sword for the first time who can't understand how to free the blade, Oslan remarked. Finally, as Oslan reached her and held Skirdkhen to her throat, she let out a shriek of, "Flanx, *do* something!"

Instead however, Flanx only cursed loudly as the queen's crown curiously stuck to his palm. After a few futile attempts to pull the circlet free, Flanx, to his credit, resumed his attempt to run at the king. Oslan thought quickly, trying to gauge who was the lesser threat. Realization dawning on him that Aurastia was not the mage after all, he turned away from her, using a fluid twisting motion that brought his sword slicing through the air to his left. There was an acrid smell of burning and then a loud *clang* as Skirdkhen dropped the running man in his tracks. Flanx fell, and the Circlet of Dalenden hit the marble floor, still stuck to his lifeless hand.

Zaltreous let loose a torrent of Almatrae, and the stone floor beneath Oslan's feet shifted, throwing him off balance and into the clutches of Aurastia, who had drawn a dagger hidden within her bodice. Aylan hurled her own spell in an effort to save them from the book, causing water droplets from the air to accumulate and splash down onto the open pages of the *Almatraek Dim*. She had hoped to make the ink run, ruining the spells within, however, the water ran in rivulets harmlessly from the unblemished pages.

Zaltreous started to laugh maniacally as he hurled another spell at Carn, who had snuck behind him. Carn lifted into the air and he hung there, shield and sword still dangling from his hands. In front of the thrones, Aurastia held the dagger to Oslan's throat while shrieking at Zaltreous. "See! This is why I wished to stay safe within my own home! Flanx is dead, my magic is gone, and everything is ruined!"

"You can't cast a wit, can you? In fact, you never had any magic to begin with, did you?" Zaltreous raged. "You thought to order me about, toying with my affections as a cat does a puny rodent, and you're not even an equal. Do you know that I was actually starting to have feelings for you? Tell me, did you ever love me?"

"Ha ha ha," she laughed, "*love* you? Who could love such an incompetent fool? I have no magic, and I am still the one who has captured the king. Now be a good boy and bring me the *Almatraek Dim*. After costing me my mage, you owe me that much."

Oslan began to calculate in his head. He could tell that Aurastia was losing it. This had clearly been Zaltreous' desire, taking over his kingdom, but it was this woman who had indirectly paid. People who stood to lose nothing else were the most dangerous to face, and currently he was incapacitated. He tried to decide whether it was a good idea to drop, possibly surprising her, but then he might possibly get his throat cut. He looked to his beautiful wife and wished that he could read her mind. Her head whipped toward Zaltreous as Carn, behind him, started making choking sounds. Zaltreous' face had turned as red as the tomatoes Oslan had admired as a boy in the kitchen's vegetable patch. The mage shook with rage, and his hands, squeezing tighter and tighter, forced his magic to bear down on the dangling knight, squeezing the life out of him.

Aylan used a new spell to seize Aurastia's hand, pulling it and the dagger away from Oslan's throat. The arm unbent slowly by degrees as Aylan's spell fought against Aurastia's physical strength. Finally, as the two women faced each other, and

Aurastia's arm was forced straight out between them, Oslan was able to lunge to the side. He spun and dropped as he did, using his foot to knock the baroness' legs out from under her. She came crashing down, her hand releasing the dagger, which was still caught within Aylan's magic spell. Oslan watched in horror as the sharp blade sailed across the throne room at an alarming speed strait at his mage's body.

Aylan dropped her magic spell, but the momentum of the dagger was already too great, and it continued on its deadly path as if thrown at a high speed by an expert hand.

Chapter 47
~ Till Death Does Part Us ~

Two arrows were loosed. Thornton came crashing through the door, bow already drawn, in time to see the dagger fly from Aurastia's flailing hand. Without wasting a moment, he aimed toward Aylan and let fly.

Oslan felt his legs buckle as his muscles turned to jelly. If he had had the time, he would have told Aylan to turn sideways to make the target of her body all the smaller. As it stood, the dagger drawing closer to its mark headed dead center toward her core.

Had the whole world gone crazy? Was this the life he had risked his neck for? Would this end with a lifetime of solitude commiserating with his mother over their losses? Perhaps he would leave this land and wander with Lazelan to put a stop to all this death.

Thorn's arrow couldn't save her. As the dagger began to rip through the fabric of the queen's dress, Thorn's arrow intercepted it, causing it to skip to the side. Both arrow and knife clattered to the ground, and as Oslan began to rejoice, the red plume of blood began to spread at her side. So then, the arrow had only shifted the knife's course.

Trembleton bounded across the throne room. He stood over the downed Aurastia with his sword pinning her down. "Go to her," he told the king, and Oslan, coming to his senses, ran to his fallen queen.

So focussed on his wife was he, that Oslan almost missed the scene playing out on the other side of the room. Frantic to save Carn, whose face was now turning an ashen blue-grey hue, Bowregard let loose his own arrow towards Zaltreous. Unlike

Thorn's though, Bow's shot never reached its target. Zaltreous snatched up the giant tome and still had time to raise his hand to fend off the attack. The arrow deflected off the space in front of the evil mage and ricocheted straight for the slackened Carn. The arrow struck the shield in the dead center of the dragon's breath bloom. Fire blazed out, engulfing the unsuspecting mage who stood in its path. Carn's motionless body fell in a crumpled heap, and the ashen quality began to leave his skin as he began to cough and once again to breathe. The unscathed book landed atop the perfect pile of ashes that had been Zaltreous, sending black flakes pluming up and out on all sides of it. They floated delicately back down, see-sawing on the air.

Oslan reached Aylan and scooped her up into his arms. She looked up into his face and tried to smile while a violent shiver racked her body. Her eyebrows knitted together. "I'm so cold," she admitted weakly.

"Quick Sire, while she yet draws breath, we must get her to the tree. She still has work to do. We must save the kingdom," Bow reminded him solemnly.

Hating himself for the necessary pain he was about to cause her, Oslan strained to lift her without jostling her about too much. She cried out in a ragged scream as the deep red spread further through the fabric of the purple dress turning it black, and Oslan felt his heart split in two. He laboured to make her comfortable upon reaching the tree. He sent Thorn to fetch water from the well and when he returned, the king ripped a strip from his own tunic to wet and hold to her skin. He tenderly brushed the hair away from her face while clinging to Xinavane's instructions.

To crack the stone, you must awaken the

tree...Only a love that blazes like the fire of the creature will let loose its scorching breath. To shatter the bark, you must first break the vine, its fierce fiery blast will the stone then unbind.

He looked up at the sorry-looking tree that also looked ready to take its last breath. The vines, previously tight, had now broken through the bark to cause little rivers of green sap to form all over the tree. The previously lush colours of the boughs had all paled and very few of the leaves remained. He bedded down upon the fallen leaves, back leaning against the trunk of the tree, cradling Aylan across his lap.

"We have to break the vine," he thought aloud. "Thorn, can you reach any?"

"No, Sire," he responded, looking up at the tall branches all out of reach. "Perhaps I could climb though." He began to scale the tree, climbing with some difficulty into the lower branches. Wherever his boots scuffed the tree, the bark sloughed off like dead skin, opening new holes in the scaly bark.

"Watch out for the sap," Oslan warned him, "It's quite painful."

"Actually Sire, I don't feel a thing," Thorn informed him as he pulled his own dagger from his boot and proceeded to cut the first vine he could reach.

When the vine snapped, Oslan knew his first presumption had been wrong. Several of the leaves still clinging to life rained down from the tree, and the lower boughs seemed to sag even further. He didn't think the tree would last much longer. His mind raced. They needed to break the vine, but that had only made the tree worse. They needed people in love and he and Aylan were here. Did she not love him as much as he cherished her? Was that the problem?   Had he hoped for too much?   They needed to break the vine. His mind spun in circles. Then he had it.   The sap burned him but not Thorn...why? Because Thorn hadn't been touched by the tree, he was not married. Oslan yanked up his sleeve and once again regarded the vine tattoo from their wedding.   It needed both of them. "Thorn, your dagger," he shouted, "and quickly!"

Chapter 48
~ A Cut Above the Rest ~

Oslan felt the ground shake as Thorn dropped out of the tree beside him. He placed the handle of the dagger into the king's palm and asked what he could do next.

"Roll up her sleeve," the king ordered. Then to his wife, who was now barely holding onto consciousness, he explained. "Aylan, it is our vines. We must cut them to awaken the tree...that has to be it." His voice trailed off, not entirely sure. He waited anxiously to see what her reaction would be, and was rewarded by the same courage she had shown years ago in the marketplace.

"Do it Oslan, let me help my people one last time." She began to cough lightly, but without much strength left, they were weak imitations of the infliction at best. Her eyes closed tightly as her body shook, and did not open again. Instead, her lids slackened, and her head lulled unconscious upon his shoulder. *Perhaps it is for the best,* he thought in anguish, *at least this way she won't feel the pain.* Thorn raised her sleeve bearing a very pale arm. The tattooed vines there seemed darker than usual, standing out against the starkness of her skin. He clasped the back of her hand in his palm and lifted their hands out, bringing their forearms together and exposing both wrists at once. Taking Thorn's sharp dagger, he clenched his jaw against the pain and sliced through the vines on both of their arms.

The ground began to rumble from deep beneath them. On the surface, Thorn was knocked off balance, and Oslan watched in wonder as all of the fallen leaves started to vibrate, almost seeming to hover above the dirt. The vines above them started writhing like snakes, and began to slither back along the boughs, leaving open wounds in the tree where they had broken through the bark with their constriction. Oslan thought it might be best to move, but couldn't bring himself to disturb Aylan, whose breathing was so shallow now that he had to listen with his ear near her mouth to make sure she still lived. He wrapped his arms tightly around her, and prepared to fend off any further harm that might try to come at them.

Moments later, the two of them were thrown apart as the mighty tree trunk split in two and the spirit of a green dragon burst free from its core. It landed on all fours in the garden, and let out a primordial roar so loud that Oslan thought his ears might begin to bleed along with his arm. It flapped its now unfurled ethereal wings twice, testing them, before rising into the air and racing off toward the Ocean Of Empathy, blowing ghostly fire upon the land.

Oslan finally understood. All hope was indeed now lost, and despair came crashing down on him as he reflected on his failure. They had freed the beast, but what had ever made them think that the dragon would want to help them? He had gladly risked his life for his people, and as his life's blood mixed with the leaves on the ground, he realized he was a good king. However, he was a poor excuse for a husband.

He crawled back to her body and held her close to him. He would hold her now as her pulse weakened, whether she knew he was there or not. He recited her name over and over, as his clumsy fingers combed through her hair and he told her he loved her. He had promised on their wedding day to love her and stay with her till death did part them, and as the end drew nearer, and his salty tears cut paths in the dust on his cheeks, he knew now that

that would not be the case. For he understood that in a few moments time when her heart could beat no longer, and she left him alone, the end of the world itself could not force him to leave her.

Chapter 49
~ A Sappy Ending ~

The ancient spirit of the dragon soared over the buildings and hills, farms and boroughs deeply troubled by what it saw. People everywhere were frozen in time, as if the sand had been removed from an hourglass and it could no longer count the seconds grain by grain. The spirit had been rudely awaked from its warm comfy nest of the tree, and knew its home had been destroyed forever unless she could bring the vines that bound it back to life.

She came to the edge of the ocean and made a smooth gliding circle out over the water before heading back inland. This time, as she headed toward her nest, she rained down fire upon all those she saw, anxious to return to the beating hearts she had left behind. She hated being out in the open, the air was too large, too empty, too exposed. She longed to be curled up once again within the confines of her boughs and leaves, vines and roots. Perhaps she would make the tree bloom again when she returned.

All that lay in the path of the dragon as she zigged and zagged across the land felt the heat of her fiery breath. The intense heat cracked the stony shell that held the kingdom's subjects captive, and bit by bit the people freed themselves, learning once again what it was to move.

The dragon progressed hastily, but made sure to do her job well, as each couple bound by her tree would re-fortify her walls. She watched, faintly amused as she saw people carrying on as if they had never stopped. A few knew. Some people, though they couldn't put their finger on it, would have an intrinsic feeling that something had happened out of the norm. Those were far and few between though, and mattered not an inkling to the majestic beast that was beginning to grow weary. As she neared the outskirts of the castle, and finally the keep itself, her fire endured, and blazed in a continuous assault until all the stone beings were freed. She could feel the heartbeats that needed her, they were young and weak, and though they could not call to her, she felt their pull. It was time for her to get back.

*   *   *

Oslan was so grief-stricken, he almost didn't register the huge green form that landed in front of him, or the shriek of fright from Thorn.

Without rising from his protective position, he screamed at it, voice cracking with his onslaught of words. "She was a good and noble person! She was my world, my reason to live, and you have helped to take her from me. Are you happy?"

"The people are safe and well," she replied non-apologetically.

"Not all of them." He flung at her in his misery, once again focusing his attention on his wife's lifeless form.

"Why do you let her bleed?" the dragon asked, curiosity unfathomably touching her intellect. "Humans think they are smart, he bleeds too and chooses not to save them," she seemed to remark to herself, or perhaps, to no one at all. "Now it is time to be well."

Her words started to sink in past the anguish he felt, and he began to feel a spark of the hope he once harboured. "How do I make it stop?" he demanded.

The dragon swung its large tail around and dipped the tip into some of the sap that ran down the sides of her broken nest. She held the tail over Aylan, and the king watched confounded, as the drop of sap elongated and prepared to drip onto the maroon bull's-eye that now decorated the side of his wife's dress.

"No, it burns!" He warned, trying without any success to move the deadweight of her form out from under the assault. Thorn tried to push the huge, muscled tail away from the fallen queen, but it did not move, and the dragon flicked him away like an annoying fly with the back of one wing. He landed somewhere amongst the rose bushes.

"No, it heals," the dragon contradicted, turning her attention back to the queen. The droplet of sap fell through the air, landing within the uncovered gash of broken skin that Aurastia's dagger had created.

Oslan was then howling as the vine on his arm blazed with a burning fire that seemed as intense as the sun. He released Aylan to roll with the pain, crushing the leaves beneath him, and covering the brilliant vine by hugging it to his chest. It was as if his old metal smith had taken a poker white with heat to carve patterns in his flesh. After a moment, when the pain's heat began to fade, he noticed how cool his hand felt. Looking down, he noticed the intensified vines only glowed to the cut on his wrist. From there to his fingertips, the vine appeared to be black and dead.

He eagerly rushed back to Aylan's side, examining the slit in the dress left by the knife. The blood remained in the garment, but her side appeared as smooth and unbroken as a perfect flat stone fit to skip across a lake.

Looking up at the giant ghostly figure, he asked "And our wrists, will they heal too?"

"By reconnecting the vines, my home will be

reformed. I must go now, I grow weary. One trip outside the nest is enough to last a hundred thousand years." With that, she leapt into the air with one last flap of her wings that sent the fallen leaves spinning in miniature tornados through the garden. She dove into the trunk of the tree with a last remark to the king: "keep them safe, she will rise to greatness."

"I know," he responded in gratitude. It was faint, but he could almost swear her heard the echo of the ancient spirit's chuckle as it sunk back into the tree.

Oslan ran to the now bright trunk of the tree, running his wrist's broken skin through the sap. Once again, his arm flashed in pain, but he ignored it, dipping the fingers of his other hand in yet more sap to bring back to the wrist of his beloved. He watched as the severed vines on their skin wove themselves back together until they appeared as if they had never been broken. In fact, there now appeared to be a tiny new leaf growing that he could swear hadn't been there before.

The tree's branches lifted noticeably, as the trunk grew back together. The vines on the tree lengthened and relaxed, once again hanging lazily over and around the healthy and brightly coloured foliage.

Hugging his mage, the king wept, this time tears of joy as he heard music to his ears – Aylan's voice once again speak his name.

Chapter 50
~ The Journey ~

Weeks and then months passed before life truly returned to normal. Aurastia, having been found to have no magical abilities of her own, was stripped of her title and jailed as a common peasant. The Circlet of Dalenden was added to the treasury that contained the royal jewels, however, it was kept far from the pillows that held those crowns belonging to the queen.

The *Almatraek Dim* was a problem. Oslan knew that Aylan had spent hours every morning trying to destroy the blasted thing, with no success. After her first attempts with fire, water, and air, she had begun to try less and less traditional means of breaching its protective spells. Each time she attacked the book, she would leave the room sickened to the point that Millie eventually just took up a post outside the room where it was locked away with a basin for the queen. It took another a month or more before Oslan's pestering finally convinced Aylan to take a break, and to leave the frustrating book alone for once.

Halfway through the morning, when she called for Millie and her basin despite having a quiet breakfast with the queen mother, she was ordered to bed while Oslan fetched her own mother to her side. He had become slightly over protective of his wife since the day he had almost lost her, and had gone so far as to wait on her personally during every one of her now frequent illnesses. He worried deeply after the now frail quality of his wife, and thought that spending time with Lorelyn might do some good.

Aylan's mother arrived and bustled into the room in a frenzy, eager to see her daughter. Taking one look at her healthy flushed cheeks, and Millie standing by with the basin, she rushed over and converged on Oslan. Hugging and kissing them both in congratulations, she left him feeling as though he had been slugged as she exclaimed "Ooh, by the shields of the army of Ormond, I hope it's a girl."

*   *   *

Lazelan walked freely through Xinavane's palace deep in the heart of the Embralic Desert. He was glad he had made it this far along his trip, but knew he had a long way yet to go. Xinavane had willingly given him many cryptic answers, but it was with her servant, Xander's help that he had truly begun to understand the information. He was glad he had found a friend in this unusual man, and he would miss Xander when he left in the morning. Thankfully, this time he would be led through the hidden exit, and shown the safest way to travel through the maze of booby-trapped tunnels within the desert's huge pyramid.

He returned to the room that had been assigned to him and laid down wearily on his low palate. As soon as he was horizontal, he allowed his eyes to slide shut. He had heard of the fate of his former best friend, Zaltreous, from Oslan. Although he was no longer a threat, Lazelan was still resigned to find the *Almatraek Bright*. Perhaps within its pages, they would find an answer as to how to destroy the *Almatraek Dim* once and for all.

His thoughts turned homeward and he worried after Magdolyn. She was alone at their cottage, and though she understood that he had headed into a difficult expedition, he had perhaps made too light of the dangers that had befallen him.

His mind continued to churn as he drifted off into a fitful sleep where he dreamt about the day he and the master had set out on this fantastic and dangerous journey.

~ The End of Book Two ~

Dear Adventurer,

Thank you for travelling again with our heroes as they crossed the Ocean of Empathy to the darkness of the Evenwood Forest. You learned that magic is more common and secretive than most of the peasants of Endalwynndale think. You stuck by our king and queen as they met Augle, the one eyed Cyclops, battled the manipulative Aurastia, and ended Zaltreous' reign of terror forever. The knights have won this battle and have made our kingdom safe once again, but beware; more evil is on its way. Fantastic creatures only ever imagined before will begin to visit the palace, and ancient booby-traps will try to thwart Lazelan's mission to find the Almatraek Bright. Join us again in, *Enchanted Page*, where you will meet Lazelan's two unlikely companions, as well as a dastardly villain who would hide his wicked deeds behind the innocence of a little boy.

Till A Quest Calls Again,

Heather Reilly